THE TWELFTH BOY

A Novel
by
MILAN SERGENT

Praise for
The Twelfth Boy

"If you love reading a novel where you can feel creepiness slowly sneaking up on you and the main characters, you'll love The Twelfth Boy by Milan Sergent. Sergent is a master at keeping readers wondering just who or what is behind the mysterious disappearance of sweet 6-year-old Noel, a boy who loves dancing, singing, and Christmas…. Sergent keeps us turning pages until the big reveal. The reveal is more than just an ugly discovery: it's a scathing commentary, even a warning about religious and social prejudices…. Yet it will leave you thinking about the ramifications of living in a Bible-oriented society that is so anti today's trends that it is destructive. Curious to find out why I say that? Read The Twelfth Boy!"

—Viga Boland for *Readers' Favorite*

"The Twelfth Boy by Milan Sergent is compelling reading. Every time I pick up one of his books I expect to be thrilled and this one did not disappoint…. The story deals with the subjects of religious fanaticism and non-conforming characters beautifully in a thrilling horror story you will be, in turn, too terrified to read yet not be able to put it down. Another great story from a master storyteller who knows how to grab your attention and keep it from start to finish."
—Anne-Marie Reynolds for *Readers' Favorite*

"The Twelfth Boy by Milan Sergent is a fast-moving, page-turning novel that took my breath away…. I read this book in one sitting, glued to the pages, and I can't recommend it highly enough. It poses many questions about our perceptions of society and the ideas we are subjected to from our early years. A beautifully crafted book that deserves to do very well."

—Lucinda E Clarke for *Readers' Favorite*

"I finished the book in a single sitting, waiting with bated breath for the dark mysteries to unfold. With a riveting storyline and a swift pace, Sergent's book will bewitch readers…. If you appreciate mysteries and are not bothered by a few unpleasant truths, this novel will provide you with a thought-provoking read."

—Shrabastee Chakraborty for *Readers' Favorite*

"The Twelfth Boy feels like a much-needed novel for our times as homophobia, bigotry, and systematic corruption still run rampant and hamper humanity from reaching its full potential…. Savannah's story will break your heart and force you to reflect upon the ills facing our society. The Twelfth Boy is a must-read, and I highly recommend it."

—Pikasho Deka for *Readers' Favorite*

Table of Contents

CHAPTER ONE

Over the orchestral hum, now muffled and scratchy, the first nine words of "Away in a Manger" repeatedly warbled across the living room. Savannah was beginning to feel a dull stinging under her stomach and right cheek—shattered Christmas ornaments that had shed with every pine needle on the tree she and her son, Noel, had decorated seven months earlier.

This would be the last Christmas tree she would ever have or care to see. She had sworn bitterly to leave it up forever, but even it had died.

Savannah had no idea how long the needle on the record player had been jumping back to the beginning. She no longer heard Noel's sweet voice singing one of his favorite songs, a song by Bing Crosby that Savannah had loved as a child. The vodka and sedation pills hadn't killed her as she had hoped. Their numbing powers were wearing off, and she was back to the wicked reality that her son was dead, and she was once again all alone.

Her vision began to clear, and her gaze followed her outstretched arm over the beige carpet. In her hand was the thing that had caused all the tragedies—if only she could blame just the elf doll, a harmless ornament for God's sake! Its crushed head a reminder of her crushed world.

She flicked a shard of green glass off the elf's red vest and would hope to everything one more time—a Christmas miracle. Her son would come dancing into the room and take the doll he loved so, and this would all fade like a terrible nightmare. With a cramping arm, she tried to lift the elf from the floor.

"Here, Noel, it's yours now. Mommy says you can touch it. Please, please take it…."

A cracking and thud sound of wood slamming against the wall dissolved the Christmas miracle. Noel wasn't there. She realized it was July.

Two black-clothed men appeared in stalking movements from behind the couch. Their guns drawn. Even this triggered Savannah's worst nightmare. One man kept his gun aimed in readiness as they knelt beside Savannah, crunching a red Santa ornament under his shoe.

"We're with the FBI." He presented his badge. "Are you Mrs. Savannah Graysen?"

"Unfortunately," Savannah thought she had answered, still face down on the floor, a place she would've been content to serve as her eternal resting place—her home—a tomb still containing the last happy breaths of her son. If only the agents hadn't left the door open, letting the outside air of harsh reality suck out the last bit of his life she tried to preserve.

"We received a call from your employer. They said you haven't been to work or answered your phone in several days. Do you think you are able to sit up, ma'am?"

Savannah tried to push herself off the floor. Her hands dug into the dry pine needles and glass. The other agent turned off the record player and rejoined his partner. Together they helped Savannah onto the couch while she clutched the elf in both hands covered in dried blood.

"She looks dehydrated. Better get her a glass of water from the kitchen," said the agent, who called her name wrong. She was no longer a "Mrs." either—a title she had waited years to receive.

Savannah thought she recognized the two agents but downed the glass of water anyway. Her blouse sagged around her breasts and stomach. She felt like she had lost ten pounds; her husband would have been proud of that at least. She must've been passed out for longer than she had realized. Her remaining neighbors had probably already taken down their Fourth-of-July banners while Savannah was still trying to cling to happier times: the six-and-a-half years she had taught Noel to love Christmas and share in the only great memories she had as a child.

The Graysens's upper-middle-class home was typical for many houses in 2019: Open floor plan, beige carpet and paint everywhere, comfortable but contemporary furnishings, and very few pictures on the walls—a Scotty

Graysen remedy against nail holes that might decrease the resale value. Except her husband had made an exception and insisted his deer heads and antlers wouldn't leave too many scars on the sheetrock. He did allow Noel and Savannah to string a few colorful lights through the antlers and pretend it was Santa's reindeer glaring at them with glassy black eyes.

Even with the sun beaming through the windows, and red and green holiday knickknacks scattered about, the house seemed so empty now, as though a cruel monster had ripped its soul from every room. Now that the nightmares were returning, she realized monsters had done just that.

Savannah didn't even care that the agents had found her prescription bottle of sedatives and the empty bottle of vodka scattered across the tree skirt. As if those two pain killers alone had formed the jolly grins on the Santa faces printed across the seasonal fabric. Grins that had once brought Savannah and her son so much joy were now the twisted grimaces of devils.

Staring straight ahead on the couch, Savannah didn't realize her fingernails had been digging into the elf until several cuts had pierced the felt clothing down to the cotton stuffing. The agents' faces sank into knowing expressions of guilt, as they sure as hell should be. They knew the system that had long been in place, and they always covered for one another.

Even the sight of men in uniforms, which she had hoped never to see again, had brought the unimaginable events of the past back into her memory—day by day—

like the sad diary she had confided in as a youth—a girl far too mature to have colored Decembers rosier than they probably ever were.

"Every lash which God then gives the sinner shall be with a scorpion, every pain which He inflicts shall be more eager than appetite, more cruel than revenge."
— Rev. Robert South

CHAPTER TWO

Savannah Purser began her dreaded journey home from Delray High School in Egypt, Alabama. Only this afternoon, she walked on the opposite side of the road just in case any of her classmates drove past her and saw the breakout of acne on her left cheek. She must have run across the street too hard; her ankles and knees began aching.

It was November 28, 1994, and despite being her first day back at school, following Thanksgiving break, it turned out to be a wonderful day. Of course, any day was great when a new hot topic around the school detracted the students from noticing Savannah, her oily hair, her weight, her round face speckled with acne. Today Savannah wasn't a monster. During lunch, all the kids were spreading the news that cannibal serial killer Jeffrey Dahmer had died in prison that morning. And earlier in the year, serial killer John Wayne Gacy had been put to death. Many students at Delray High were just starting to realize the extent of the depraved individuals hiding among society but also that consequences and justice often came far too late.

Savannah got chills when she allowed herself to think about these dangers. The day she was born, the famous mass murderer and preacher, Jim Jones, had died. Savannah's parents, Molly and George Purser, said evil had been purged from the Earth that day because their sweet little angel had come down from Heaven and into their lives.

Molly and George had never prepared Savannah for the harsh realities of adult life. Everyone should cling to childhood—the boundless joys of knowing that even Santa Claus was looking out for you all year to reward you with lots of gifts under a tree on which you helped hang sparkling tokens of hope and joy. All Santa needed in exchange was a plate of yummy cookies, which you get to eat most of before promising to stay in bed and not peek until morning came. And then there was the tooth fairy, who made losing a tooth an absolute thrill while you imagined how you'd spend the money she left under your pillow. At the Purser house, the Easter Bunny never failed to leave baskets of candy and chocolate and prized eggs all over your yard. Even Halloween was a delight, putting on a mask of your choice for one night and filling up your pumpkins with every candy imaginable. But you controlled the scariness of it all.

The only holiday that Savannah didn't enjoy as much as other kids was Valentine's Day, especially the older she got, when the only hearts she received were from her parents at home. Images of every girl and guy in her school parading around, comparing their cache of cards and roses were too harsh of a reality, especially when everyone obviously judged her worthy of nothing. More than anything, Savannah wanted to change this. She wanted love and to have a hot boyfriend carry her around like a trophy and make all the lucky girls jealous for once.

It didn't take Savannah long to realize that evil hadn't gone anywhere and that she wasn't special. Her younger brother, Jeff, had been loved by all—both girls and boys. He was handsome, good at sports, and made better grades. He died a year earlier after playing with his father's hunting rifle. Jeff didn't know the gun was loaded. That's the problem with life, Savannah realized; you never know when something or somebody is loaded and about to go off. She would never have been jealous of Jeff if she'd known he would die so young. She had thought about killing herself many times since that day and just might if she thought anyone but her family would miss her.

A car slowed down near her, and the booming bass rattling the hood and trunk softened. Savannah recognized the song by Kurt Cobain, who had also died this year, but it wasn't celebrated, not at her school anyway.

"Oh, God, it's Carl," Savannah mumbled under her breath and snapped her neck straight ahead, slowing her stride in case her flab jiggled too much. She had the hots for Carl the minute she had seen the quarterback in his gold jersey, and his white pants stretched so tight, she could see the elastic bands of his jockstrap cradling each of his firm butt cheeks and his more important area. He looked like a true angel with his wavy gold hair and tan, but Savannah couldn't possibly be "sweet sixteen," not with thoughts like this. Her heartbeat raced when Carl Fortenberry leaned out of the driver's window. He was right beside her now.

"Yo, Savannah Banana! I'll bet your parents hafta keep four spare tires in their trunk to haul you around. Ha-ha-ha!" chuckled Carl, followed by the cackles of at least five other guys crammed into the car with him. One of the boys threw a half-eaten chicken leg, which smacked against her aching kneecap, leaving a grease stain on her torn blue jeans. Thankfully, Savannah tried to fit in with the Grunge kids so nobody would probably even notice the stain. But she knew it was only a look—a way to hide. Behind the sheltering walls of her home, she liked everything happy and colorful, especially at Christmas, for which she had already helped her parents start decorating.

Clutching her schoolbooks and trudging straight ahead, her skin grew feverish, and she got an instant headache. She let her long hair fall over her face because she had become so self-conscious of her every movement that it was hard to walk. She could easily see herself collapsing on the sidewalk in front of her entire town. Only two more years of high school, and she would never even consider going to college. Her parents would let her live in their house forever; they had to.

Her achy and swollen joints didn't go away the following week, so her mother took her to two different doctors, and the diagnosis was lupus, a systemic autoimmune disease.

"Keep taking your medicine and omega-3, and maybe it'll go into remission, at least for the holidays anyway," said Molly in her Southern belle accent. She steered the SUV home, careful not to mess up her Santa-themed nail designs. "But you really should start eating better."

"Whatever. Even when I was skinny, boys never noticed me." Savannah crumpled against the car door window, which was thankfully tinted dark.

"Oh, now, honey, don't go getting all doomy and grungy on me—isn't that what you kids call it these days?"

"Not! It's called doom and gloom," sighed Savannah.

"Try and perk up. 'Tis the season to be jolly, after all. We can still make all our Christmas cookies. You know how much you enjoy that." Molly carefully patted her daughter on her knee and turned on the holiday music: Blue Christmas. She quickly muted it. "Oh, darn! I scratched a nail." She shoved her fingers in Savannah's face. "Does it look like 'Yo! Ho! Ho!' now?"

Savannah turned to look at her mother. "But what if I don't ever find love, Momma? I don't want to be alone forever."

"You can always try what Grannie Jones taught my mother. Oh, never mind; it's not politically correct for the grimy girl generation."

"Not! It's called Grunge," Savannah reminded her mother.

"Okay, 'Grunge.' I hate that word. But I won't have my daughter accusing me of going down on the wrong side of history. I can't get you to talk to me as it is."

"Wait. What did Grannie say? I swear I won't report you or none of that." Savannah wiped her hair out of her face; both were already so oily she was sure her eyeshadow and mascara had melted down to her cheeks.

"She said to find a man, you have to do your hair and makeup every day—no exceptions—no matter if the trend is to look like a backwoods holy roller trapped in a polygamy cult. Then you need to become a great cook and learn how to dote on your man—let him be the ruler of the castle."

Savannah realized her eyes had enlarged, and she was still gawking at her mother. "As if! God, that all sounds so 1950s." Savannah feared some old scrub wouldn't even choose her as a sister wife, no matter how gross that seemed.

Molly frowned regretfully and then looked in the rearview mirror to fluff her big hair. "See, I warned you. It's not all of this grungy, seven-year bitch kind of carrying on—not for the long haul. Most men like sweet girls— feminine girls—whether they show it or not."

CHAPTER THREE

Eighteen years of loneliness and depression had passed, and Savannah had become a noteworthy cook, winning six first-place and two second-place ribbons in a county fair contest. She won, namely for her barbeque, but her homemade cakes were always in demand. She rarely tasted her cooking; she was determined to keep her weight and lupus under control. She was beyond relieved that she had finally found love and was convinced it was from having cosmetic surgery and skin resurfacing.

On Valentine's Day in 2012, when she was thirty-three, she married Scotty Graysen, a man she had met at one of the county fairs. He made such a scene over her "killer" barbeque ribs that the fair employees had threatened to toss him out. Savannah laughed. They thought Scotty was drunk.

With a ring now on her finger, she couldn't believe she might consider attending her first high school reunion, just to let her former classmates see what they had overlooked—let them drool over the hunk of a man who wanted her in every way. And Scotty was far better looking than that Carl *Farten*berry, who had shown off his Valentine's roses shoved down the back of his tight white jeans, like Morrisey did in the "Heaven Knows I'm Miserable Now" video. And she hoped the former quarterback was miserable after the way he destroyed her young life.

Scotty, who had worked selling sports cars for years, bought his own car dealership in Birmingham, Alabama, and together he and Savannah purchased a light-brown brick home there in the city. The front yard was medium-sized but well-landscaped. A wooden fence hid the backyard, and it had a party-sized swimming pool, which Savannah could only use in the evenings because the sun usually worsened her lupus. The square footage of the Graysens' home at 221 West Dawson Cove was not as expansive as most on the street, but it was more than they needed, especially since the doctor had told Savannah that her health would prevent her and Scotty from having children. Scotty wasn't thrilled with the news but refused to consider adoption.

The first week after they had moved into their new home together, a middle-aged woman, with light-brown hair teased into a helmet, knocked on the door and introduced herself to Savannah.

"I just wanted to welcome you to the neighborhood! Do you have children?" the woman asked, clutching one of the twelve crosses on her necklace while peering left and right through the doorway, then down at Savannah's ring finger.

"I have little time for that. I'm finishing up my online degree in bookkeeping. I'm going to work for my husband's car dealership."

"Uh-huh. I see. The Good Lord intended women to stay at home and attend to their husband's needs, you know? Oh, how presumptuous of me." The woman grabbed Savannah's arm. "Perhaps you and your husband don't have a church home yet." She reached inside her beige purse. "Y'all need to come to ours. I happen to have one of our cards right here—"

"I hate to cut things short, but I've got a casserole in the oven." Savannah shut the door.

The woman slowly knocked twelve times on the door. "Behold," she yelled from the outside, "the Lord stands at your door and knocks. If you hear His voice and open it, He will come in to you."

After finally completing her online degree, Savannah worked at home for Scotty's car dealership, which gave her time to rest some to prepare him good suppers when he came home and fulfill his needs in the bedroom. Anything to keep him as she was taught.

"Something smells delish," he said, hugging her from behind that Saturday afternoon. He patted her stomach. "You putting on a little weight there, babe?"

"A little, I think, but—"

"You know I prefer my women like my cars. I'm into a speed-sort-of-build and not comfort. Hold on, babe, and I'll show you." Scotty walked out of the kitchen and soon returned with the swimsuit edition of one of his sports magazines. He flipped toward the middle and ripped out a page featuring a big-breasted beauty with blonde hair down to her narrow waistline. And this he secured carefully to the refrigerator with four tiny car magnets.

Shaking now, Savannah slammed the stirring spoon on the oven. "Here; you can serve yourself. Enjoy your meal, and I'll go throw up. Will that make you happy?" She wiped the tears from her eyes on her dress sleeve, stormed off to her bedroom in her high heels, and locked the door. With her face smearing makeup on her pillow, she waited for hours, hoping to hear an apology through the door, but it never came. Just the sounds of a rerun baseball game poured from the living room at top volume.

What if she couldn't stop gaining weight? Would Scotty leave her?

Savannah cried herself to sleep.

The next morning, she awoke, feeling unwell. She threw on her robe and headed toward the kitchen to find some stomach medicine, passing her husband, who was still asleep on the couch.

"Oh, gosh," she gasped, and clasped her hands over her mouth as she mazed through the house, hoping to make it to the bathroom in time. She had just lifted the lid on the toilet when she began vomiting. One of her heels had come off in the hall in her rush.

"What the hell are you doing?" asked her husband, appearing in the doorway in his boxer shorts and tank top. "Look, I wouldn't've said anything if I thought you'd try and become anorexic. I didn't think you meant it about puking and all."

Savannah hid her face from Scotty. She didn't want him to see her sickness or smudged makeup from last night. "I'm sorry. I didn't throw up on purpose. I haven't been feeling right, that's all, my love. It might be my lupus. I'll make an appointment with the doctor for Monday if she can fit me in."

"That woman? She sounds like a quack. You should find a real doctor. Anyway, I'm taking the boat out and do some fishing. Do you need anything before I get back?"

"No, thank you." Savannah pulled her legs together properly under the toilet bowl. "You go and catch the biggest fish in the lake, and I'll fix you some barbeque ribs for supper. You will be home for supper, won't you?"

Scotty drummed his fingers on the doorframe, and then his lips shifted into his famous playboy grin and wink. "Well now, I might have to cut my trip short for a mess of those ribs."

Early Monday afternoon, Savannah rushed home in a daze. Her lupus doctor had recommended she buy a pregnancy test from the nearest pharmacy. It couldn't be true; the doctor had assured Savannah months earlier that such a thing wasn't in her future.

She left her keys in the steering wheel with the engine running but reached back into her car and got them. Trying to unlock the front door to her home, she dropped the keys. Finally inside, Savannah kicked off her heels and bolted to the nearest bathroom while holding three different pregnancy kits.

She had felt like a sexual deviant at the pharmacy counter, especially when the pharmacist said the tests were cheaper by the dozen. "Still," the man added, after handing her back some change, "the price of sin is great."

With shaking hands, she read the instructions before urinating on the white test sticks all at once, which surely wasn't the wisest thing to do.

Savannah washed her hands and held her breath as, one after the other, the tests all read positive. She double-checked the results with the instructions and got tingles from her toes to her forehead.

"Oh, my gosh. Oh, my gosh!" she repeated, wandering through her house, panting for air as if she had just run a marathon. How should she tell her husband the fantastic news? Her mind raced with clever ideas until she just couldn't stand it any longer, and she fished her cellphone out of her purse and automatically dialed the first number in her list of favorites.

"Look, babe, I'm in the middle of a huge sale right now. Is something wrong?" asked Scotty.

"Scotty, we're going to have a baby!"

"Look, Savannah, I don't have time—"

"Scotty, I just took three different tests. I'm pregnant."

"Are you shittin' me?"

"Dr. Tao suspected it first. That's why I gained a little weight. I saved the tests so you can see."

"Hot damn! Yeah! Yeah! My wife's having a boy!" Scotty yelled and whooped, while some employees in the background cheered. "I'm on my way home, babe. Take it easy, and I'll be there in a few minutes. I love you."

"But I haven't had time to prepare dinner."

"To hell with dinner. I'll order delivery from every restaurant in Birmingham if I have to."

CHAPTER FOUR

Scotty wouldn't stop bragging to his friends that he was having a hunting buddy one month and a fishing and sports buddy the other eight months of their pregnancy. Savannah had feared otherwise. So, she was more overjoyed than Scotty after giving birth to a healthy baby boy. The greatest thing of all was their baby boy was born on Christmas Eve. This couldn't have pleased Savannah and her parents more. It was a sign: Heaven had gifted the world another one of its angels.

Savannah got her way with Scotty for a change and named him Noel.

The first six years were magical at Christmas, and little Noel always enjoyed singing every Christmas song he knew the words to, especially "The First Noel," which he thought the angels had written about himself. But he preferred the songs about Santa and his elves.

During this time, something about the holiday season brought out a warmer, playful side of Scotty, which Savannah hadn't seen earlier. Scotty would have Noel right by his side on "the boy's couch" as they watched old holiday classics on television. Every year before bedtime, he would read "'Twas The Night Before Christmas" to his son and speak in a deep jolly voice as though he was Santa.

One Christmas Eve, after Noel was fast asleep, Scotty rushed into the living room and began doing the thing most parents dreaded, assembling toys and hoping the boxes contained all of the parts. He had put together most of Noel's first bicycle, which was lying on its side near the tree with presents and tools scattered around it. Making a quick grab for the rubber grips to put on each handlebar, he stumbled over his drill in his bare feet, and his stomach landed on the exposed metal of the bike's right handlebar.

"Argh!" Scotty yelled.

Savannah jumped up from the floor where she was wrapping gifts. "Oh, gosh, Scotty. Are you okay?"

"I think so, other than impaling myself," groaned Scotty.

Rubbing his sleepy eyes, Noel came into the living room in his pajamas. "I heard a noise," he said, before noticing the mess around the tree and Savannah helping Scotty off the bicycle. Blood dripped down the handlebar and had soaked through Scotty's white t-shirt. He grabbed the wound with his hand.

Scotty looked up at the ceiling. "Is this my punishment for having a little fun with my son? Huh?" he growled. His face reddened with anger or pain; it was hard for Savannah to tell.

"Oh, nooo. What happened?" asked Noel, about to cry.

"Your dad came in the room when Santa was putting your gifts under the tree and accidentally ran into one of Santa's reindeer. One of its horns got him," said Savannah, so Scotty wouldn't have to strain to talk while he remained bent over in pain.

"You going to hospital, Daddy?" asked Noel; his little hands covered his face as though he was getting a fever from concern. "Is Cwistmas gone bye-bye?"

"No, sweetie," said Savannah. "We're going to get Daddy to the North Pole to see Santa, and he'll make everything all better again."

Noel's eyes enlarged. "Santa Claus can fix anything?"

"You bet he can. Now go back to bed," said Savannah, putting her arm around Scotty and helping him to a chair in the kitchen.

Once Noel's personality was beginning to develop, Scotty began pulling away from his son. Savannah knew the best time to bring this up with Scotty was after the two of them had sex. He was always his most tender and attentive during those moments.

". . . Oh, here we go again. I've tried, babe. Noel doesn't like to do anything I like to do," said Scotty, pulling the bedsheet over his loins and rolling over.

Savannah turned on her side and spooned him. "Not every boy is into killing animals and kicking other team's asses, Scotty."

"Ah, there you go again, tryin' to make me look

bad—tryin' to turn Noel against me. It's called huntin' and sports," said Scotty.

"It's like you don't really want to be with Noel anymore, so you're just going to play the rejected parent and be done with him." She kissed his shoulder, hoping to keep him calm.

Scotty pulled away from her next kiss. "All normal boys wanna be like their fathers." He sighed and pretended like he wanted to sleep.

Savanna rose on the bed. "Sweetie, you're a fully grown man, and he's not even seven yet. You haven't made one effort to get to know Noel and his interests. You can't beat him all the time and expect him to follow you around like a puppy dog."

Scotty shoved his fist into his pillow and buried his head deeper into the soft foam. "I was wondering when you were gonna use that against me," he grunted. "All kids need spankings, Savannah. But you'd rather coddle him and let me be the bad guy."

"Why don't you stay home this weekend, and you and Noel can put up the yard decorations and lights—just the two of you. It would mean so much to him."

"I already promised David I'd pitch him a few balls. You know how important it is for him to make the Little League next spring."

Savannah turned off the lamp. She had a sinking feeling it was more important for Scotty that his ten-year-old nephew made the baseball league. She resented that her sister-in-law couldn't get her own man to help raise her son. Of course, she wouldn't need to with Scotty driving down to Tuscaloosa all the time. Always something needed fixing there, or a pine limb that needed to come down. And naturally, Scotty always got pulled away longer than expected. He always told the same story: his nephew wouldn't take "no" for an answer and needed help learning to master a different ball or shoot a "real" deer—something with enough antlers to hang his ball caps, jockstraps, and helmets on.

With Thanksgiving days away, and Scotty at his sister's place, Savannah showed her son how to string red-and-white lights around the wire sculpture of a life-sized Santa Claus in their front yard. An icy breeze circled them on occasion.

"Oh, Mommy, c-cold wind means Santa's coming soon. *Hn-hn-hnn*, my ears are freezing off," Noel said with a hum of a giggle, pressing his hands against the sides of his head and raising his eyebrows goofily.

"That's because you have big ol' elf ears." Savannah pinched his nose and pulled his Santa cap over his ears to match the position of her cap.

Still giggling, Noel grabbed the red lights and began to dance around the sculpture while singing "Rudolph, the Red-Nosed Reindeer."

He paused on the fourth loop when a group of neighborhood boys stopped on the sidewalk and yelled, "Sing, Noel! Sing."

Noel fidgeted for a few moments while the boys snickered. His smooth brow creased, and tiny nostrils flared, while the string of lights in his hands quivered.

"Come on, Noel. I think we should go back inside for a bit," whispered Savannah.

Noel didn't budge. He held his head high and continued with the song, dancing around the sculpture, slow at first, then with unrestrained jubilance.

"Noel is a queer!" the tallest boy shouted, while other boys yelled worse.

"You sound like a dying dog," shouted the fattest kid in the bunch before he let out a howl.

Noel's lips clamped into a slight frown. He dropped the lights on the dead winter grass. Savannah could see his little chest throbbing through his coat.

"Um, you stop that, okay!" he yelled back at the boys. "I'm, um, going to be an elf in my s-school musical. And, and you'll see!"

"Aw, come over here, little elf, and let me punch ya in the nose."

"Yeah!" the other boys sneered, pumping their fists

into their hands.

"He looks more like a fairy. Go and cry to your mommy, little fairy!" said the oldest boy flapping his hands limply.

Savannah reached out to pull Noel into the house and thought she was hallucinating. Stacy Beachum, the next-door neighbors' son, came dancing into their yard in fur-lined boots, candy-striped stockings, and a lime-green ballerina skirt bouncing under a military-style camouflage jacket. Stacy was six years older than Noel, and the two boys had only waved at one another on occasion. But Savannah had never seen him dressed as a girl before.

Stacy and his parents lived in a two-story beige-stone home with two chimneys, a circular drive in front, and a high-angled architectural-shingled roof, which Savannah had seen Stacy playing on at least three separate occasions.

Stacy stopped twirling when he had reached Noel's side. With a graceful lift of his arm, he gave the middle finger to the group of boys while holding in his other hand a plastic Halloween pumpkin full of makeup, candy, and toys.

"It's the icepick killer," said the tallest boy to his chums, before they turned and ran down the road, yelling more insults.

"Yeah," Stacy yelled at the boys, "come near us again, and I'll stick ya!"

"Are you okay?" Stacy asked Noel, shoving his fists on his hips, deep into his fluffy skirt. "I'm Stacy Beachum, and you are Noel Graysen." He held out his hand in a welcoming gesture.

Noel seemed extremely curious as he eyed Stacy from his wavy chin-length hair, his multicolored fingernails, and lastly, his black boots. He reluctantly reached up to shake the boy's hand.

"Too late; bad fate," sang Stacy. Instead of shaking Noel's hand, he twirled his fingers three times and shoved his fist into his camouflage jacket.

"I didn't know it was you at first, and, um, that's all," said Noel, touching and tugging on his cheeks while most of his teeth flashed in a grin. "Um, are you a girl or boy?"

"It depends on my mood. Mostly I'm just Stacy."

"Noel needs to get back inside now. We have lots to do today," said Savannah. She took Noel's hand and pulled him toward the door as his eyes remained fixed on the weird neighbor.

Savannah didn't know what the boys meant by calling Stacy "the icepick killer," but she didn't like the sound of it at all. Stacy was definitely of age to be in school, Savannah realized. But she had never seen the child leave the yard since the Beachums had moved into the neighborhood a year earlier.

"I don't want you going anywhere near Stacy—ever. Understand?" asked Savannah, closing and locking the front door.

"Why? What did she, um, do, Mommy?" asked Noel, with his usual little gasps of air between words.

"For one thing, Stacy is a he, and another—you need to play with kids your age—that's what." As soon as she built up the courage, she was going to try and have a talk with Stacy's parents.

"But I don't got any k-kids my age to play with," said Noel lifting his arms in frustration. He twisted his fingers together and then lifted his arms victoriously. "*Hn-hn-hnn*," he giggled. "And, and I'm going to go to the North Pole and, um, be friends with all of Santa's elfs, and you can come, too. Have the elfs brought my c-costume yet, Mommy? My teacher Ms. Casey she, um, said I'm going to be the elf in the Christmas play this year."

"They're called 'elves' when there's more than one, Son. Ms. Casey said you *might be*. But you have to audition first." Savannah didn't want to shatter his hopes, but it was too soon to buy an elf costume. Even if his music teacher did choose Noel for the lead part, Savannah knew he would wear out his costume before the musical even began.

CHAPTER FIVE

Sunday morning, Noel decided it was safest to play in the backyard where no one could see him through the tall wooden fence. His parents were still in bed asleep, so Noel knew this was the best time to start working on something special for his parents for Christmas. He took out his coloring pencils and drawing pad and began making them a pretty card. He drew his fondest memory of his daddy lifting him up to hang the angel on top of the Christmas tree while his mommy watched them with a plate of cookies she had baked to eat. He made sure he left a few cookies for Santa later. Noel wondered if he should give them their card on his birthday, Christmas Eve, or wait until after Santa had come. Several minutes later, he couldn't think of anything else but Ms. Casey picking him as the elf in the musical. He closed his sketchbook and began practicing his singing and dancing, but not too loud because he wasn't supposed to wake his parents.

On the grass several yards from the covered swimming pool, he leaped and crossed his legs for the third time before landing on his bottom.

He raised up and saw something red and white, like a candy cane. Whatever it was, it pulled back through a hole in the fence that divided his house from the Beachums' house.

Noel got goose bumps. Maybe it was an elf coming to bring him his costume, he wondered. Breathing hard, he crawled toward the fence on his hands and knees and saw that the candy cane wasn't real candy; it had a magnifying glass on the tip. He peeped through the lens and saw an eyeball blinking back at him.

"It's me, Noel! I, *hn-hn-hnn*, know who you are. You d-don't got to hide or anything."

A few seconds later, a rope ladder dropped down from the other side of the fence. Noel waited for the elf to climb down to his side of the yard but realized the elf must be shy, so he climbed the ladder to the top of the fence and looked down into the Beachums' yard for the first time.

"Hello, Noel!" said Stacy, face-to-face, while rising from a trampoline he was bouncing on. Today Stacy was wearing baggy white pants, with dog collars binding the fabric to his ankles, and a t-shirt with big red lips and the words "The Rocky Horror Picture Show" on the top. Stacy's lips were deep blue, and his hair was slicked down to his head.

"Wanna see my treehouse?" he said, rising in the air again.

"Where is it?" asked Noel.

Stacy bounced back up and pointed to his left at a giant sprawling oak. "In the tree. Where do you think treehouses are supposed to be?"

"I can't becuuuuz I'm not allowed to talk to you," said Noel, placing a finger under his bottom lip.

"You're already talking to me, elf boy."

"How did you know I'm an elf."

Stacy jumped off the trampoline and walked toward the tree. "I can't hear you way over there."

Noel thought Stacy was the coolest person he had ever seen, and he always wanted to go inside a treehouse because that's where lots of elves live, so he sat on the top of the fence until he built enough confidence to jump down onto the trampoline. After about ten bounces, his feet landed on the ground, and he ran under the canopy of branches which made half of the yard darker. A huge bucket covered in fake flowers lowered from the tree by four ropes. Noel opened the door and stepped inside the bucket, which began to lift back into the tree.

When the bucket came to a stop, Stacy was waiting on the other side of a swinging bridge connecting to the bestest treehouse Noel could imagine. Hidden by billions of leaves deep within the branches was a house bigger than Noel's whole bedroom. And it looked like Santa had built it out of candy and flowers of every color.

"Wow!" laughed Noel, easing across the swinging bridge. "You don't live up here, do you?" He curled his fingers above his ears and flashed his bottom teeth.

"No," said Stacy, opening the door shaped like an ice

cream cone and stepping inside. "I only come to Stay-City to play games and write in my diary. Sometimes I like to sing—like you do. I named my treehouse after myself. Could you tell?"

"Yeah," Noel giggled, though it took him a few minutes to figure out it rhymed with his name. "Why did those boys call you a, um, icepick killer?" he asked, sitting beside Stacy on a furry orange rug. With contorted movements, he looked around the treehouse. One whole wall had shelves crammed with video games, books, board games, and a black hat with a rounded top. One polka-dotted wall had old posters of somebody named Boy George, and a poster of Grace Jones, and two of a band called Dead or Alive. Cool people who kinda looked like Stacy. Behind Noel was a closet full of costumes and over their heads was a spinning ball with lots of tiny mirrors, which made little balls of light sparkle and dance around the room. Only a little natural light came through two stained-glass windows like a church Noel had gone to once.

"They kept beating me up at school, and the principal wouldn't help me. So, I hid an icepick in my lunch bucket, and I stabbed one of them in the leg. I didn't kill him. My whole school thinks I tried to, though. My dad is a psychologist and kept me from going to jail. I just have to be homeschooled from now on, and those bullies get to keep on terrorizing others until they actually do kill somebody."

"Aw, why did they beat you up?" asked Noel. He frowned bigger than usual, so Stacy would know he supported him. "Is it 'cause you wear dresses sometimes?"

"It's against the rules for me to wear dresses at my old school. I guess they beat me up for wearing a little makeup and for being different. My mom is from India, so I'm what they call mixed here in Alabama. They also called me names like they called you. I get bored playing by myself now, so I peek through the fence a lot and see what other kids are doing. I figured out you like elves."

Noel realized that Stacy had protected him against the bully boys in the neighborhood. "*Hn-hn-hnn*," he laughed and slapped his hands against his grinning cheeks. "I think you look super-duper cool." He tried to remember some of the bad names the boys had called him. "What does q-queer mean? Is that what they, um, call elfs at your school?"

Stacy frowned. "I'm older than you. So, you should probably let your parents answer that question, or they might get mad at me. But it's okay to be whatever you want to be here in Stay-City. Someday, I'm going to turn this into a clubhouse for only fun people and no bullies. I might let you be my first member. But you will have to have the special key to get in." Stacy pointed to a shoe-sized key hanging on the wall above the door; it sparkled with every color of the rainbow.

"Ooh, it's so pretty," said Noel. "It looks like candy."

"I made it myself, but you can't eat it. I do have some real candy." Stacy fished a colorful candy sucker out of a skull jar and offered Noel the jar to select his own piece of candy.

Noel plucked an orange sucker out of the skull and

realized he had better return to his yard before his parents came looking for him. He had learned never to make his daddy mad. Noel always cried and begged his daddy to stop beating him with a belt. He knew his daddy loved him, but still, he wondered why Scotty's face changed when he was mad—like he wanted to kill Noel—like the bad daddy he saw in a movie called "The Shining." Too, Noel didn't know why his mommy never came to save him.

"You had better be a good boy and not make Daddy angry, or Santa won't bring you presents anymore," Savannah would always warn Noel.

"Thanks. I had fun." He stood up and hugged Stacy, who jerked back with wide eyes before his blue lips formed a more natural smile.

Stacy lifted his wet sucker like Noel had seen adults do with wine glasses. "Here's to new friends."

Noel looked at his orange sucker. What if he got Stacy's spit on his candy?

Stacy leaned his head to the side. "I don't have cooties or anything."

He touched his candy to Stacy's and giggled, "Friends, *hn-hn-hnn*."

Just before Noel climbed back over the fence, Stacy leaned over the railing of his treehouse and shouted, "Hey, elf boy! If you want to be the first member of Stay-City, I can make you a key."

"Okay!" Noel laughed.

CHAPTER SIX

Savannah sat in the auditorium of Susan M. Neeley Elementary School, where Noel was in first grade. She held her breath, awaiting the music teacher, Casey De Grasse, to announce which students would be playing the main parts in the Christmas musical "Santa Needs New Helpers."

A woman leaned forward and tapped Savannah on the shoulder. "Your boy has a pretty good voice. He shouldn't listen to a word the other children say about him. Some boys are just—you know . . . dainty."

"I train my son to pay no attention to jealous kids," said Savannah, biting her tongue not to say something nasty in return.

The woman tapped Savannah's shoulder again. "My son is the third from the right. He's hoping to play Santa. But I'm not so sure I want him in this musical. I mean after all the reports about the teacher, Ms. Casey."

"What reports?" asked Savannah.

"You mean you haven't heard? At least three parents have accused her of being, you know, a little touchy-feely with their kids. That's how it all starts, they say."

"All I know is Noel just loves Ms. Casey. I think the trouble with a lot of children these days is a lack of physical affection—truth be known," replied Savannah, who decided to switch to the next chair, farther away from the woman. She had felt like the biggest reject her whole life in school, and she was going to support her son no matter what it took to make him happy.

"Well, that's what's turning all these boys into queers and sissies these days," said the woman, loud enough for Savannah to want to punch her.

"Everyone, please be silent as I make my decisions," said Casey into the microphone at the center of the stage. The rows of children behind her were squirming more than ever. Noel couldn't keep his hands still as usual, and he kept pulling on his little face. He waved at Savannah at least three times during the tryouts. That was what probably set off the woman in the seat behind her. Her son never waved, and twice he shoved any kid who happened to stand in front of him.

Casey lifted a sheet of paper near her face. "If I call your child's name, please wait until the end of the selections, and I will hand each of you a list of costume requirements in order to help make this year's production more magical than ever."

A short woman with her brown hair piled high on her

head stood up and lifted her hands toward the ceiling. "We don't need magical. Jesus is the reason for the season. This is the fifth year now. You are trying to take Christ out of schools. What's wrong with just having a traditional Nativity—Mary and Joseph and a manger scene?" The woman mumbled some gibberish, which Savannah took to be something called speaking in tongues.

A dozen or so people clapped and said, "*Aman.*"

Casey fumbled with the sheet of paper in her hand and adjusted the microphone. Her throat and upper neck turned pink. "Feel free to address any of your concerns with Principal Harmon. Everyone has an opinion as to what he, she, or they prefer, and so I ask you once again to not turn this harmless children's event into a personal protest."

"'They!' Did you hear that?" spat the woman, smacking Savannah's shoulder with her fingertips after moving over one seat closer to her. "All of this gender-inclusive nonsense."

Savannah tried to ignore the woman as Casey announced the selections:

"For the lead elf, I have chosen . . . Noel Graysen."

Giggling, Noel flailed his arms wildly and grinned bigger than Savannah had ever seen. She batted her eyelashes, trying to dry her tears of joy before her mascara ran. Such a little thing to make him happy, she realized.

"And lastly, for the role of Santa Claus, I have chosen . . . Tina Moore. Congrats, Tina."

Applause broke out as Tina, one of the oldest girls on the stage, received a few hugs from her friends.

"HO-HO-HO!" Tina laughed in a deep voice, sticking her belly out for laughs.

"You. Have. Got. To be kidding me!" huffed the woman behind Savannah. "She picked a *girl* to play Santa."

As everyone began to leave the auditorium, Savannah turned and slapped the woman's shoulder, the way she had done to her several times. "You shouldn't take it to heart. Sometimes choices are made according to talent and not tradition."

As Noel came running up to Savannah, she could feel the woman scowling at her.

"*Hn-hn-hnn*, I did it, Mommy. I'm an elf!" He hugged his mother as hard as he could. "Maybe my costume will come soon."

Casey pushed through the crowd and stopped in front of Noel. She patted him on the head, messing up his dark-blonde hair, causing him to laugh even more. "Mrs. Graysen, I'm so glad to meet you finally. I just want to say how thrilled I am to have Noel this year. I think he is going to be one of the best singers this school has ever had. He's certainly one of the most enthusiastic. I see so many other kids, and I know they want to take singing, acting, and dancing seriously—well, they just need more good influences like Noel here."

"Thank you, Casey. I think you just made my son the happiest elf on the planet," said Savannah, taking the sheet of paper from her with the costume requirements.

"The happiness of the elect in heaven will in part consist in watching the torments of the damned in hell. And among these it may be their own children, parents, husbands, wives, and friends on earth."
— Rev. Nathaniel Emmons

CHAPTER SEVEN

Savannah and Noel placed the red-and-green-sequined pillows on the couch for extra holiday cheer. Noel had picked them out in the home décor store earlier that afternoon and thought they couldn't live without them. He had also seen an elf doll that he went nuts over, but Savannah decided she would wait and get it for his birthday, which was four days away.

With the Christmas play just two days away, Savannah was relieved to finally get an email notification that Noel's elf costume was finally out for delivery that afternoon. She had contacted the seller and had made several nasty complaints after the seller claimed that they had already shipped it two weeks earlier, along with a list of other contradicting excuses they gave her.

Noel was getting on her last nerve. He had been checking under every piece of furniture in their home, looking for where the elves had left his costume. Before and after school, he had patrolled the bushes in the front and back yard like a dog sniffing out a mole.

"Maybe they left my costume on the roof?" asked Noel.

"Don't you even think about climbing up there," huffed Savannah. She lowered the meat fork she was wielding and tried to think of an excuse while preparing dinner for Scotty. "Sweetie, elves never leave presents on the roof because they might get wet if it rains. That's one of the first things they learn in Santa's workshop. They're probably taking their time to make your costume extra special."

"Maybe they left it at Stacy's house. Can I go over and see?" Noel pressed his chin to his shoulder with a coy look.

"We already discussed this. Your father doesn't want you to ever speak to that—to Stacy ever again."

"But he, he didn't kill anybody. He was just trying to keep the other boys in school from hurting 'im," said Noel.

Savanna found herself wielding the meat fork again. "You went over to Stacy's house after we told you not to— DIDN'T YOU?"

"Yes, ma'am," Noel said, lowering his chin to his chest.

"Wait until I tell your father!"

Noel broke into sobs. His quivering arms lifted to swipe the tears gushing down his red cheeks. "Please don't t-tell Daddy. Stacy's very nice. He, um, let me play in his treehouse and, and he gave me some candy."

"I've talked to his parents. I know all about Stacy. He's very mixed up no matter what they say. He's been banned from attending school. Now, just go to your room," said Savannah.

Minutes later, feeling as guilty as hell, she thought she heard the UPS driver backing out of her driveway. She dried her sweaty hands on her apron and opened the front door. There on the concrete by the potted topiary was a package. She opened it to inspect the elf costume. It looked perfect. She could deny Noel the only friend he had made so far, but she couldn't deny him this elf obsession he had developed, not when she had fostered it because of her own love of Christmas. Savannah folded the outfit back as neatly as possible and placed it on the floor in the pantry and called for her son, who eased back into the kitchen, looking around with puffy red eyes for his daddy.

Savannah tried to add a little cheer and softness to her voice. "I'm not sure, but I think I saw an elf sneaking out of the pantry. Why don't you look and see if he left your package there?"

Noel's glassy eyes enlarged, and he crept up to the pantry and peeped through the door.

"It's here, Mommy! *Hn-hn-hnn*, I got my costume!" He ran toward her and then shuffled his little legs back toward the pantry.

"Well, put it on; let's see."

Noel jerked at his sweatshirt until his head finally cleared the neck opening. He took off his sweatpants and tried to squeeze his little legs into the green tights, stumbling backward onto the floor in the process. His face heated red, and his mouth twisted with little whines. Savannah knew that she should feel the same excitement, but her heart felt like something was squeezing it. Noel's joy seemed somewhat unnatural, as if he were desperate to disappear behind the costume. Perhaps she had just forgotten what it was like to be almost seven; she did have him at an older age than most women, after all.

Savannah turned the cooktop temperature down on the oven and helped Noel into his elf outfit.

It fit him perfectly, from the red-and-white floppy cap to the red vest, green tights, and pointy-toed shoes.

"*Hn-hn-hnn*, I can't wait for Daddy to s-see me. Oh, he's gonna be so excited," giggled Noel. The little bells on his shoes and hat jingled as he went leaping toward the bathroom to check out his reflection in the mirror. Distant squeals and laughter assured Savannah that she had ordered the perfect costume. She braced herself against the kitchen counter when her arms and legs went limp. She couldn't tell Scotty that Noel had gone to visit Stacy, not now.

Throughout dinner that evening, Scotty kept his elbows on the table, chomping on fried chicken. He hardly looked at Noel, who was still wearing his jingling costume, keeping particularly quiet.

"Anything happen at work today, dear?" asked Savannah, trying to break the ice.

"My employees bitched 'cause a couple of their atheist coworkers got Christmas bonuses like they did—ain't' ever happy."

"Here, let me get you some more tea," said Savannah, reaching for the crystal pitcher.

"I see you two've been busy today," mumbled Scotty, with a mouthful of wild rice.

"We went shopping," said Noel, swaying in his chair. "I picked out Cwistmas pillows. They're pretty."

Scotty grunted and wiped his mouth with his napkin.

Savannah tried to keep grease from dripping onto her new burgundy dress, which was not easy when she was more worried about keeping the mood light and breezy instead.

"Um, Daddy, I learned all my parts for the musical. I can do 'em for you before you come to my school tomorrow." Noel lifted his white elf collar over his chin.

"Jesus, Savannah. You didn't tell him?" Scotty glared at Savannah over his fork speared with lettuce.

"Noel, you hardly touched your supper. Why don't you go to your room and watch television?" said Savannah, wanting to have a private discussion with Scotty.

"Okay. And I, um, can practice some more before tomorrow." Noel slid out of his chair and danced to his room.

"Of course I didn't tell him, Scotty! You know I can't do that to him. He's had his heart set on us both being there to see him sing."

"It's time he grows up and stops all of this—"

"All of this what, Scotty?"

"Jiggling around in those green pantyhose for one thing," he groaned, and tossed his chicken bone on his plate.

"They're tights. And he's only six, for God's sake. *You* tell him you'd rather go hunting with your nephew. *You* tell him you're afraid he's turning gay because he still believes in Santa like most kids his age."

Scotty shoved away from the kitchen table, and his chair scuffed the tile floor. He tore into the living room, grabbed the sequined pillows off the couch, and held them up like they were some sort of contraband.

"And what is this, Savannah? What is this? Disco pillows?"

"What is with you, Scotty?" She tried to pull the pillows out of his hands, but he lifted them above his head. "You're being such a macho knucklehead these days. If those same sequins were on a dress I was wearing, you'd go on and on about how you loved it. You'd be ready to take me to a diner party. But on a pillow? On a pillow or curtain or now on a Christmas tree, you act like you'll go up in flames. I don't get it."

"I don't wanna see my son wearing it, though," Scotty mumbled through pouty lips. "I don't want my house turning into a sissified disco. He's already got boy band poster all over his room and those Harry Styles—hairstyles—or whatever you wanna call 'em books."

Despite Savannah pleading to stop, Scotty threw the pillows across the room and knocked a signed art vase off the bombe chest, shattering it and scattering sequins.

"Just calm down with all of this Christmas shit, all right?" Scotty pressed his palms toward the floor repeatedly. "It's time we tell Noel the truth. Maybe give him a chance to become a man."

"Make him bitter, miserable, and paranoid as you? Is that what you want?" Savannah finally saw right through Scotty. "You want Noel to grow up faster because you think his preciousness is just a baby thing and not really a part of his nature. We don't have any guarantees he might not have the same personality long after he reaches puberty. Noel might not show it, but it hurts him that you'd rather have your nephew for a son."

They both froze when they saw Noel standing with a long face and teary eyes at the edge of the hall leading into the living area. He turned and ran to his room.

"Now you've done it. Are ya happy, Savannah?"

She placed the pillows back onto the couch and pointed her finger in Scotty's face.

"Don't you hang this on me!" Savannah whispered, spitting accidentally. "You're gonna get your sorry ass to his Christmas musical, and you're gonna tell your son how proud you are of him if you have to say it through gritted teeth." She stomped out of the living room, hoping she could undo everything that Noel had overheard. She finally got what she wanted, a husband and a child, but never in a billion years did she expect to be dealing with this situation so late in life.

*"Be afflicted, and mourn, and weep: let your laughter be
turned to mourning, and your joy to heaviness."*
—James the Apostle (KJV)

CHAPTER EIGHT

Noel's big night had begun. Savannah and Scotty were sitting about ten rows from the front—as close as Scotty felt comfortable. He slid low in his chair with his legs spread and arms folded. The lights in the auditorium dimmed, and the stage curtains opened, revealing an elaborate stage with Santa's workshop and a closed sign nailed over the door. Music started playing, and before long Noel came leaping across the stage singing, "I'm a little elf, yes I am, and Santa needs help; he needs a helping hand. . . ."

A young girl sat down in the chair next to Savannah. She crossed her legs, and Savannah noticed her clunky black heels poking through the bottom of her long coat that had a scrambled modern art print. Despite her jet-black sunglasses and blonde wig styled to look like large mouse ears, Savannah was sure the girl was not a girl but Noel's forbidden friend, Stacy.

Stacy waved at Noel when he stopped singing and

dancing. Noel's face lit up, and he gave a small wave back. It was as Savannah had feared; Scotty craned his neck to the right and tensed when Stacy waved at him and Savannah, lowering his dark shades and batting his purple-glittered eyelids.

"You invited that freak, didn't you? How could you?" Scotty jumped up and stomped out of the auditorium, leaving Savannah sitting there with Stacy and everyone watching. She was worried sick that Scotty, in his rage, might leave them stranded at the school, but she couldn't—she wouldn't dare miss the rest of Noel's performance.

Scotty wanted to spit bullets as he stomped through the elementary-school hall, heading for the entrance. He had never been so humiliated in all his life. How would he explain this to his staff at the car dealership, who already question Scotty why he doesn't have photos in his office of his boy playing sports or holding up a dead fish, turkeys, or something Scotty liked to hunt? He punched open the glass door with one hand and fished his cigarette pack out of his coat pocket with the other.

On the concrete steps underneath the bright security lights sat a young man or teenage boy, it was hard to tell with his white overalls and backward baseball cap, and he was smoking a cigarette as well. He nodded at Scotty, who gave a reluctant nod back before leaning against the brick entry and taking a few pissed puffs. He couldn't believe he had given up his hunting trip with David for this. It was all David had wanted for Christmas, not some look-at-me, dancing-around-in-green-pantyhose school play with a girly-boy freak cheering him on. He should have listened to the others. Marrying Savannah had been a big mistake.

How could Scotty think such a thing? He still loved Savannah, but he was going to have to get tough with her and Noel. His eyes became moist, but he refused to look like a Nancy boy about it. Maybe he *should* sell everything and take them out of the city, back to the Garden of Eden where women knew their place under men, and men had no unnatural influences except to hunt and garden. Where their only duty was to offer sacrifices to God in exchange for the bounty He provided. The only problem was Scotty couldn't bring himself to offer up his firstborn son, and Savannah was too attached to Noel and this perverted world.

The young man stood up and flicked his cigarette like he was giving the finger to the world. He walked over to Scotty.

"Was that your boy—the elf?" he giggled. "Yeah, I saw you coming into the school with him. He's a peppy little kid. Peppy." The young man kept sniffling his nose and twitching his neck.

Scotty tried to change the subject. "You're a little old to be in this school, aren't you?"

"Ha-ha-ha. I'm just the janitor—*custodian* everyone's forced to call it these days. Like it makes a difference for the old wallet, right? Yeah, I'm waiting to clean up the stage, that's all. It's a real shame what they're making kids like your boy do in there—goes against everything in the Bible."

Scotty tossed his cigarette and grabbed the boy by the bib of his overalls. "Who do you think you are, you little punk? Don't you say a word about my son. Got it?" He shook the boy, who smirked and rolled his eyes back as if the threat had aroused him. This gave Scotty the creeps. He released the boy, who picked up his fallen cap and took off running down the darkened street, giggling.

"The twelfth knock will be your last, Scotty Graysen," the boy yelled from a distance.

How did the little punk know Scotty's name? The whole school must be gossiping about the Graysen family. Well, they can't blame Noel's effeminate behavior on the father like they usually do, Scotty figured, grinding his teeth.

He wanted to take a scalding shower; the whole night had been shitty. And now he was going to have to endure a guilt trip from his wife and son. He smoked a few more cigarettes until people started leaving through the doors where he lingered.

Savannah and Noel walked through the door and

paused on the top of the steps, looking for Scotty.

When Savannah spotted her husband, she gave him the dirty eye, just as he expected. Scotty knew this was his signal to brag about Noel's pantyhose jiggling.

"Did you see me, Daddy? Everybody stood, and they clapped."

"Um, yeah," mumbled Scotty, trying to avoid Savannah's glare. "Yeah, you really did it, didn't ya?" He patted Noel on the shoulder but removed his hand fast when Stacy came prissing through the door and stood between them.

"You are a movie star now, elf boy," smiled Stacy through his purple lipstick, making Scotty want to clobber him. He looked around, hoping people weren't staring at his son and the girly boy.

"*Hn-hn-hnn*," Noel giggled and clasped his hands on either side of his gaping mouth. "I d-didn't know you were coming to see me. You invited Stacy, Mommy?" He hugged Savannah's waist.

"No, I did not," huffed Savannah, making sure Scotty heard her. But Scotty still didn't believe this wasn't all a setup. He locked eyes with Principal Harmon, who seemed shocked to see him at the school.

"I knew you'd get the part, Noel. You practiced so hard. I saw you leaving your house in your cool costume, so I talked my dad into dropping me off here. It feels a little weird being back here. I wore a wig so nobody might recognize me." Stacy patted his blonde mouse ears. "I couldn't miss seeing my friend perform; could I? I texted my dad; he'll be driving up to get me soon." Stacy looked over his shoulder. "Oh, that's him now. Well, congratulations! Oops, I almost forgot." Stacy reached into his plastic pumpkin and removed a rainbow-colored key. "Just as I promised; you are now an official member of Stay-City."

Stacy leaned over to hug Noel and give him the key, but Noel pulled away, his eyes fixed on his father's scowl while Scotty called Stacy just what he thought of him, but not loud enough to get the crowd riled up on one of their politically correct crusades.

"Hey! I thought you wanted to be the first member of my special club," said Stacy, lowering his sunshades with confused eyes. His painted lips plumped into a pout.

Savanna jerked Noel's arm, pulling her son away. Noel's cheek dimpled regretfully, and he lowered his chin to his elf collar, much to Scotty's relief. His boy would thank his dad for this someday when he outgrew this nonsense. And come his next free weekend, Scotty decided he was going to put barbwire on top of the wood fence between his yard and the Beachum's yard, whether the city allowed it or not.

Stacy spun around and swished down the steps. Before he climbed into his father's long silver car, he yelled, "Too late; bad fate, elf boy."

Noel remained quiet all the way home in the car—peaceful quiet—natural quiet. Scotty knew his boy would come around eventually. And as soon as the holidays and all the "HO-HO-HOs" were over, he was going to make some changes around the Graysen house, even if he had to send Noel away to some type of boot camp for boys—

the Christian one with the Bible gun camp, he had learned about online, was probably best.

When they got home, Scotty followed Noel to his bedroom.

"Are you going to read me a Cwistmas story like you used to, Daddy?"

"No, Noel. I want you to get on your knees and pray. You're gonna do it every night from now on. Pray God will take away any unnatural desires and make you the man you need to be."

Noel dropped to his knees and folded his hands together as Scotty showed him. "What are unnatural dires?"

"I said 'desires,' They are things you like and want which aren't right for men, like costumes and all these posters of boys in your room—things that don't please God."

Noel's lips curled down, and he bowed his head.

CHAPTER NINE

That Sunday, Scotty had left before sunrise to spend yet more time with his nephew, which was fine with Savannah; she was still mad at him for the way he had shown his butt at Noel's most anticipated event. She read a religious pamphlet somebody had stuck on her door. It gave a brief history of how, during the sixteenth and seventeenth centuries, true Christians in America and England enacted government bans on sinful Christmas and all of its foods, music, and decorations, thus temporarily putting an end to the pagan ritual.

Savannah was stunned; she had never heard of this ban in all her years of celebrating the holidays. But the part of the pamphlet that made her skin crawl was it said her family was going to suffer in the flesh and in Hell for perpetuating the lie of Santa Claus and thereby perverting the birth of Jesus all over again.

She searched the pamphlet for a church address or affiliation, but whoever left it had scribbled over it with black ink. She tossed it in the trash and went into the living room. Sitting on the couch, she began stroking Noel's hair as he leaned silently against her with distant eyes and red cheeks. He claimed he didn't feel well, but Savannah worried that Noel was finally at the age that his little brain and emotions were processing the rejection his father was now heaping upon him.

She kept the television on something she hated: football. Of course, Noel wanted to watch the Christmas shows that were on, but Savannah was hoping he might take an interest in sports if only to appease Scotty. He just stared at the Christmas tree instead, with his hand curled under his chin.

Savannah knew she needed to give Scotty an ultimatum and make him show some affection to Noel, especially if he refused to spend time with him. But this was something she had never really tried and certainly not something her parents had raised her to do. She had this sick feeling Scotty would stop loving her as well. How would she get through life without him? No man would want her now that she was older. If only she had given birth to a girl instead, perhaps she would've had more confidence in how to raise her. Society was okay with girls singing, dancing, and shopping. And surely Scotty wouldn't've been able to bring himself to beat a doe-eyed little girl with a belt for giggling too much or being caught playing with Savannah's makeup. She was going to have to find a way to keep some things concerning Noel secret from Scotty until she could work on them both a little more.

"Son, have you made any male friends at school?"

Noel shook his head and looked down at his bare feet.

"Surely, some of the kids in the musical liked your performance. The audience clapped for you."

Noel shrugged his shoulders. "My tummy hurts."

"Sweetie, you know it's okay to talk to me about anything. Did something happen at school?"

"One of the boys in the play, he, um, shoved me and called me a bad word."

"What word did he use?"

Noel's eyes became moist, and he lowered his head again. "Umm, it's a, uh, bad word like they call S-Stacy. And, and I don't wanna talk about it."

Savannah was sure it was a slang word to accuse boys of being gay. But she had never seen her son so uncomfortable, so she decided to change the subject, especially since she feared his answer. And if anything, he might just be confused. Noel was far too young to know what he was.

"Don't worry, sweetie. Kids say stupid stuff all the time. He was probably jealous that you got the best role in the play."

"Then why can't I be friends with Stacy? I don't like the other kids." Noel crossed his legs and started slapping his hand against the couch cushion.

Savannah felt so helpless now. How could she add to Noel's worries by pressuring him to be something he might never be, especially because of Scotty's insecurities? She was going to have to lie like the rude religious pamphlet had accused her and Scotty of doing. Or did her husband put the tract on the door to stop Noel's and her love of the holiday? No, that couldn't be right; Scotty thought religions were social-club money pits. Then again, he used to love Christmas.

Savannah put on a fake smile and ruffled Noel's hair. "Your dad and I just want you to make friends with kids from your school."

CHAPTER TEN

Christmas Eve morning had finally arrived, and Savannah opened the door to check the mailbox. Today was also Noel's birthday, so she hoped at least one of the kids from his school had sent him a card. Her heart sank; the mailbox on the outside wall was empty, but when she started to shut the front door of her house, she jumped sideways. Somebody had smeared blood down the doorframe. Why hadn't Scotty noticed it before she did? She couldn't get the police involved, not on Christmas Eve. Besides, it was probably one of the neighborhood kids trying to ruin Noel's special day. She rushed to the kitchen, grabbed a rag and bucket filled with water, and scrubbed the blood off the doorframe. Just as she managed to rinse the last bit of blood off her hands, Noel came moping into the kitchen, still in his Santa pajamas. His hair had twisted all over his head from a restless sleep. Without saying a word, he sat at the table to eat his soggy bowl of cereal.

Savannah couldn't stand it anymore; Noel had been sulking around the house ever since he had lost his only friend. She dried her hands and led him to the Christmas tree in the living room.

"Now, I'm going to let you have a peek at your birthday present before your Daddy gets back from the store. But we have to keep it a secret from him, okay?"

"Oh, yesss!" Noel agreed. His eyes matched the sparkling lights on the tree, and his whole body vibrated with anticipation.

"Close your eye," said Savannah, before reaching around the backside of the tree and removing the elf doll ornament she had vowed to get him the very moment Noel had seen it in the store. It looked almost identical to how Noel had in his musical.

"Happy Birthday, sweetie!"

Noel eased his fingers from over his eyes, and his mouth sprang open as wide as possible. "Ohhh, Mommy!"

"Look. What is this the elf is holding in his hands? Could it be a birthday card just for you?" She had wedged the card between the elf's plastic hands and had angled its arms up.

Noel took the elf with twitching fingers and cradled it to his chest as though it was a newborn baby. He looked at the card.

"What does it say?" asked Savannah.

"The elf says, 'I, um, p-picked this card for a very special boy. Happy Birthday, Noel!'" Noel squealed with excitement and bent his knees as though he might pee on himself.

"You can pick a name for him, but you mustn't touch him until Christmas Day," said Savannah. By having her parents attend the party as backup, she was hoping that Scotty wouldn't make too much of a scene over Savannah getting Noel the harmless elf.

She took the doll away from Noel. "I'm going to put him back behind the tree until tomorrow. Now, remember: if you touch him before then, he . . . might get really sick."

"Oooh, I won't, Mommy. I promise."

"Now, stay in your room and think of the best name for your elf while I get everything ready for your party."

Savannah's elderly parents were set to arrive from Egypt, Alabama, in two hours. Noel was always excited to see his grandparents since he never saw Scotty's father enough to bond with him. Come to think of it, Scotty never seemed to form a bond with his father either. Mr. Graysen was a crusty, no-nonsense tractor mechanic who raised Scotty and his four siblings after their mother died in her mid-twenties. Mr. Graysen's main philosophy in life was, "If you spare the rod, you spoil the child." The problem was the man, like Scotty, found it all too easy to spare affection and interest in their children. Surely there was more to good parenting than just keeping your kids from dying physically.

To keep Scotty from getting upset about anything, Savannah was determined to be on her sweetest, most wifely behavior. She finished frosting the birthday cake and covered it with a glass covering until the right time.

The slamming of the front door signaled that Scotty

had arrived back from his last-minute shopping. During those rare "gift-huntin'" excursions, he always went with at least four or five male buddies, "the git-'er-done pack." He wouldn't dream of shopping alone or with just one friend so nobody would think he was gay. Heaven forbid.

Savannah smiled. She found it hilarious, watching those grown-ass men spread out, at least arm's distance, while barreling through the mall as if their boots were filled with fire ants and concrete.

"There you are. Did ya nail something?" she asked, while Scotty rounded the corner into the kitchen with an armful of bags.

"Yup, and you're probably not gonna like it."

Savannah knew at once what Scotty was referring to: the long black barrel of a gun was jutting out of a sporting goods' bag. She put the box of birthday candles back in the cabinet while her heart nearly stopped.

"Scotty, please tell me you didn't buy Noel a gun."

"It's just a pellet gun. I had one when I was Noel's age."

"I don't care! You know my brother died from playing with my father's gun." Savannah couldn't imagine what her parents would think when they saw Noel with the weapon.

Scotty pulled the gun from the package and loaded a pellet into it. "These tiny pellets are practically harmless. It's a hell of a lot better than that damn elf you got Noel."

Savannah turned her back to him. Icy chills traveled over her.

"Didn't think I'd see it on the back of the tree, did

ya?”

"I won't stand for him having a gun." Shaking, Savannah grabbed the barrel of the gun, which Scotty wrestled from her, accidentally pulling the trigger. With a loud *POP,* followed by the sound of breaking glass, Savannah jumped back. The cake cover had shattered.

"Oh, no!" She dashed over to the kitchen table. Tiny shards of glass were now covering the entire cake. "Look what you've done! You've ruined Noel's birthday cake." She began sobbing.

"I can't help it if panty-waisted emotional problems run in your family. Me getting my boy a gun ain't the problem. Better than you turning 'im into a pansy."

Scotty placed all the gifts except for the gun in the back of the kitchen pantry.

"Enough! I've had enough of you. You are so cruel," cried Savannah into a dish rag.

Scotty aimed the gun at Savannah with a look of rage darkening his face. He lowered it when she clutched her heart, stunned that her husband, the man she said "I do" to, would ever do such a shocking thing.

"I ain't staying for the party. I'm going to give this beauty to my nephew. He'll appreciate it. But that elf had better be gone when I get back."

After the front door slammed, Savannah sat in the chair and inspected the cake she had worked so long to prepare. It was unsalvageable. For a minute, she had a vision of a bride and groom wedding-cake topper appear on the cake before the happy couple fell into the frosting glistening with broken glass.

"What party?" she cried, still hearing her husband's last words. She collapsed on the edge of the table. Savannah had nothing to give Noel for his birthday now. She couldn't have her parents see her an emotional wreck—see that Scotty had bailed out on them—see the glass that would take longer to clean up than there was time left for them to arrive.

She pushed away from the table and grabbed her cellphone to called them before it was too late.

"Mom? Listen—oh, you're turning on the freeway, you say? Mom, you and Dad are going to kill me, but you have to go back home—no, no, I swear everything's fine. It's just, I, uh, I've suddenly become sick. I think Scotty caught something from me—yes, yes, I'm sure." Savannah coughed into the phone. "I'll catch up with you some other time." She turned off her phone. Now, how in the heavens was she going to explain that there would be no party to Noel?

Unable to face her son with the truth, Savannah decided to lie like hell to him.

"Grandma and Grandpa can't be here. They came down with the flu suddenly. Your daddy has gone off to check on them and make sure they get back home okay. They said to tell you they love you and they're sorry they missed your special day."

"That's okay," said Noel in a disappointed voice. He didn't even look up from the paper he was drawing something on at the foot of his bed.

This pierced Savannah's heart more than if he had pitched a fit. Was Noel so used to disappointments that he had lost his fight, his passion? Savannah's love of birthdays and Christmas had lasted long after her first year of school. Somehow, she was failing miserably in continuing this tradition with Noel.

"Well, Santa isn't sick, and he's going to bring you some awesome presents. So, no sneaking out of your room tonight."

Noel didn't respond at all this time. He switched colored pencils and continued scribbling away on his drawing pad, so Savannah gently shut his door.

Alone, four hours later, she placed the wrapped gifts under the tree and had given up on Scotty returning home for Christmas, if at all. She left only the tree lights on and went to bed.

An hour later, she heard some yelling which sent her heart galloping. She flung the covers off, wrapped a robe around herself, and ran into the living room just in time to see Scotty throw Noel to the floor, where he began sobbing.

"No! I wasn't gonna t-touch it, Daddy."

Scotty's dilated eyes settled on Savannah victoriously. "I caught him touching this damn elf you got him, Savannah. It's the middle of the night, for God's sake, and he can't stop obsessing over it. I told you to get rid of it. See what you're doing to him?" He shook the elf he had ripped from the back of the tree.

Like a beaten puppy, Noel went crawling on his hands and knees back to his room.

"Don't you ever throw Noel around like that ever again. You're drunk! Just leave, go back to your sister's."

"You've become a real bitch these last few years—ain't no woman ever talked to me like that. And look at ya; you look like ten miles of detour," Scotty mumbled. He threw the elf on the floor and stomped on the doll's face, crushing it. He picked it up and threw it in the kitchen garbage can. Opening the front door, he turned around with a wicked snarl. "I ain't coming back—ever."

Savannah listened as Scotty's white truck cranked, revved a few times, and squealed out of the driveway. What had she done? She had just lost her husband. Perhaps she should have seen Scotty's side of the argument. Maybe she was turning her son into an obsessed sissy. She dabbed the remaining tears from her eyes with her robe sleeve and eased into Noel's room. He was curled into a ball under the covers. His room was pitch black except for the light seeping through the door from the hall.

She placed a hand on his side.

"Son, I'm sorry your daddy lost his temper. He's not coming back, so I need you to be strong for Mommy. Santa, the elves, none of it is real. It's time to be a man now and focus on other things."

Noel didn't respond, but Savannah could feel him breathing. Perhaps he was still traumatized by what had happened and needed to sleep.

CHAPTER ELEVEN

With a throbbing crick in her neck, Savannah rolled over in her empty bed. Too much sun was coming through the window. "Oh God! I must have overslept." She looked at her alarm clock, and it was nearly noon Christmas Day. Noel couldn't possibly still be asleep.

Her hands began to tremble as she threw on her robe. Surely, she didn't leave Noel all alone on the biggest day of his year. She then remembered what she had told him around midnight. What if he doesn't even want to open his presents now? She flung the bedroom door open and ran into the living room, expecting to see lots of crumpled and ripped Christmas wrappings, but everything was as she had left it before going to bed.

"Noel!" she called out to him, but no one came running. She headed down the hall to his room. His door was open, but he wasn't there either. She dashed through every room in her house only to find them empty of life. She went into the back yard and lastly into the front yard.

"Noel!" she screamed. Surely Scotty didn't come back in the middle of the night and take him. Not when he would rather be with his nephew.

She returned to his bedroom before she saw something that caught her attention. On his nightstand, under his Troye Sivan poster, was a card folded to stand up. She grabbed it and looked at the image on the front. Noel had drawn his father lifting him to the top of a Christmas tree to hang the angel he must have remembered from a few years back.

She opened the card, and Noel had written a note in red pencil. She sat on the edge of his bed, trying to decipher all the misspelled words and scribble.

"Aw, what are you trying to tell me, baby?" Sweating, Savannah bowed over in gut-wrenching frustration. Noticing a discoloration on his blue pillowcase, she touched the area and realized the pillow was cool but wet with tears.

About to vomit, she looked up in his closet; his elf costume wasn't hanging on the rod. "Why?" Carrying the card with her, she ran into the kitchen and checked the trashcan. The elf Scotty had thrown in there was missing as well. She stumbled to her bedroom, grabbed her cellphone off the table, and speed-dialed her husband.

"Of course!" He let the phone go to voicemail. She waited for the beep, afraid she would explode and not even be able to talk coherently.

"Scotty, Noel is missing," she panted. "He drew us a

Christmas card and left it beside his bed. I, I can't understand everything he wrote here, but he said he wasn't trying to touch the elf. I think he was trying to put the card he drew in the elf's hands as a gift for us, like the birthday card I put in the elf's hands for him—from us. He got the elf out of the garbage, and his elf costume is gone, too."

The voicemail stopped recording, so Savannah dialed 911 and told the dispatcher the same story.

"Try to remain calm, Mrs. Graysen, and we'll send an officer there at once."

Savannah threw on some proper clothes and headed straight to the Beachum's home next door. Maybe Noel had gone to visit Stacy. For once, she hoped to everything he had.

The front door cracked open about four inches and Stacy's mom, Anaya, peeped through the opening just above the security chain.

"Mrs. Beachum, oh thank heavens you answered the door! I'm so sorry to interrupt you on Christmas Day, but Noel is missing. He didn't happen to come here, did he?"

"Nooo," Anaya replied in a squeaky voice. "Noel is not allowed here. You said so yourself."

"Can I please speak to Stacy? Maybe he's seen him. You know how kids are," Savannah said in a friendlier tone, hoping Anaya wouldn't judge her prejudices, not at a time like this.

"Hold on, please." Anaya closed the door and, after two minutes, eased it open again. "Stacy has not seen Noel. And, sorry, he doesn't care to see your son anymore.

Sorry."

Anaya closed the door, so Savannah returned to her property and, with her cellphone by her side, she paced in circles on the front driveway, looking for the police.

From the far end of West Dawson Cove, sirens began to wail, and blue lights flashed until a police car parked in the driveway. Window curtains parted across the street at two houses while two officers came trudging up to Savannah.

"Have you noticed any signs of forced entry?" asked the tallest of the two men, who took notes while the other officer began looking around for evidence.

"No, but the front door was unlocked from the inside," said Savannah, as she led them inside her home. She realized she was clutching her fingers in front of her chest like Noel often did when he was nervous. "Do you think he left home on his own?"

"We need more information first. Can you tell us everything that happened prior to your son's disappearance, Mrs. Graysen?" asked the same officer.

Savannah tried to relay everything in the correct timeline. Still, she held back on telling the officer about Scotty aiming the gun at her, shooting the cake cover, and attacking Noel before leaving them for good.

The officer lowered his notepad and sighed.

"Are you sure there isn't anything you aren't telling me, Mrs. Graysen? Why did your husband leave and not come home to be with his wife and child on Christmas Day? He can't be working; no car dealership I know is open today."

While Savannah thought of an excuse, the other officer walked up, holding a transparent bag.

"I inspected the trashcan where Mrs. Graysen said her husband threw the elf doll and found a bunch of shattered glass. I got a sample for forensics."

"I don't know where my husband went—to his sister's home probably. We are separated now," said Savannah.

"Mrs. Graysen, I think there is more to this story here. Why would your husband throw an elf doll in the garbage on top of broken glass? A doll you intended to give Noel for his birthday."

Savannah took a deep breath and confessed everything, including Scotty attacking Noel before crushing the doll's head.

The officer's lips squeezed in a heavy expression before he took the slightly crumpled Christmas card from her. Savannah stretched her hands toward the card.

"You aren't going to keep that? I mean, my baby did make that for us."

"I'm afraid this card might be evidence," said the officer, while the other cop searched Noel's room.

"I tried to read his writing. He just turned seven yesterday."

"Who is Noel's English teacher, Mrs. Graysen?"

"A man at Susan M. Neeley Elementary School. Noel called him Mr. Dan; I believe. Why?"

"He might be our best hope of figuring out what your son wrote in the card. Mr. Dan might be able to compare it with your son's phonics tests."

"Yes, of course! But Noel wasn't very fond of English class, I'm afraid."

"We'll also see if his kindergarten still has any of Noel's phonics tests on record."

Savannah felt loads more hopeful. "Oh, thank you. Maybe they can tell me what the card says."

"You must understand that your husband is a suspect now, so we must ask you to avoid mentioning anything we have discussed today. Let us handle everything," continued the officer.

"You can't blame him! I mean, Scotty wouldn't do anything to Noel—nothing bad."

"With all due respect, ma'am, from everything you have told us here in this report, your husband already has."

Savannah bit her bottom lip. "Well, uh, please don't make it look like I reported him."

"It sounds like he might be a danger to you. Would you like for us to arrange police protection for you?"

"No, I don't think that'll be necessary," Savannah lied. She feared Scotty's wrath more than ever now.

"All right, ma'am; we're leaving now," said the shorter officer joining them. "We'll issue an AMBER Alert for your son."

"Thank you, Officers. Please let me know the second you find him."

Savannah started to get in her car and drive the streets to look for Noel but paused. What if he came home while she was out? She closed the door but couldn't bring herself to lock it. What if he couldn't get back inside his house when he did return? She found herself wandering around every room, retracing every footstep she remembered her family taking. The house had never been emptier. It just didn't make sense. This was something she never imagined happening, especially on this day.

Savannah couldn't bring herself to look at the Christmas tree, the abandoned gifts under it. Needing all the emotional support she could get, she held her cellphone close to her bloodshot eyes. She was going to have to call her parents and admit she lied about Scotty and her being sick—admit her failed marriage to an abusive husband—and worst of all, acknowledge that Noel, their only grandchild, was missing.

CHAPTER TWELVE

Savannah sprang up from the couch in the living room when her cell phone rang at three in the morning. Her mother and father, who had come to stay with her, snapped awake on the guest couch.

"It might be Noel," stammered Savannah, fumbling to answer the phone. "Hello? Hello, this is Savannah?

"Yes, that had to be him then. Are you sure? Nobody else saw anything? Okay, okay. Thank you. Goodbye."

"Is everything all right, dear?" asked Molly, Savannah's mom, squeezing beside her on the couch and slipping her arm around her.

"News about Noel?" asked George, her father.

"The police just got an anonymous report from a woman who claimed she saw a boy about Noel's age walking down the interstate in an elf costume around 4 AM Christmas morning. She said he was holding what looked like a doll."

"Anonymous? That was nearly twenty-four hours ago. Why didn't she report this the minute she saw him?"

asked George; his arms shook so hard that Savannah thought he was going to have a stroke.

"The woman claimed she'd been to a party, drinking, and feared people would think she was hoaxing another Santa sighting."

"At least that's something to go on. They're going to find him; don't you worry," said Molly.

Savannah's chin began to quiver with the vision in her head. "I can't imagine my baby wandering down the interstate all alone at night—through all that traffic. He must've been terrified."

"A decent person would've stopped and gotten that boy off the interstate and brought him to the police station," huffed George.

Savannah pulled her blanket over her. "Noel knows our address and phone number. If somebody had picked him up, then surely, they would've at least contacted me or the police—somebody."

"Unless they're a thug. This goddamn county is full of 'em these days—no respect for human lives, nothin'."

"Now, George!" snapped Molly. "There's no need to upset Savannah unnecessarily. We have to stay positive."

Growing less optimistic by the hour, Savannah buried her face in her blanket and wailed.

"Oh, now look what you've done," Molly fussed at her husband, before pulling Savannah to her bosom. "Shhh, honey," she whispered. "Your dad didn't mean to upset you. He just loves Noel and wants him back home safely."

"I'm afraid Noel has run away," Savannah whined

under the blanket. "This reminds me of the last thing I said to him when he was curled up under his bedcovers right after Scotty—after he lost his temper. I told Noel his daddy wasn't coming back. I did a bad thing. I let Scotty get in my head, and I thought maybe he was right that I might be turning Noel gay somehow."

Molly pulled away slightly and peered through the bottom of her bifocals. "By teaching him to love Christmas? Oh, Savannah, you can't be serious. Did you turn out gay? Your father still loves Christmas and everything that goes with it, and he's as manly as they come."

Savannah blew her nose into a tissue she had been holding. "Then, after Scotty said he wasn't coming back, I thought I needed, you know, to prepare Noel—make him strong enough to handle everything. I told him that Santa and the elves weren't real."

"Before he even got to open his presents?" asked George with a grimace.

"Oh, I'm such a horrible person. No one should expect a first grader to be a man."

"From Scotty's idea of a man, you mean. Oh, honey, I'm afraid some of this is my fault," said Molly, patting her on the back.

"What do you mean?" asked Savannah, lowering the blanket to her wet chin.

"Do you remember asking me how to find love when you were a teenager—when you were convinced you were doomed to be single forever?"

"Yes," said Savannah.

"I told you that you should learn to cook and do everything you could to please a man. Always let your husband have his way—"

"A lot of fellows were like that when I was in the Marines," said George. "They wanted to marry some damn doormats with big tits."

"Yeah, but you were beautiful, Momma. You didn't have to worry about being an old maid." Savannah dabbed her eyes with the tissue one more time.

"Looks have nothing to do with it, honey bear." Molly's eyes wrinkled with a sympathetic smile. "My mother tried to put the same nonsense in my head, but she used the Bible to hammer it in. During her generation, women were to be completely submissive to their husbands' every command. But with some men, it's a disaster waiting to happen if no one stands up to them, especially when children are involved. You never told us that Scotty was becoming more abusive by the day."

"I'll kill him if he ever lays another finger on my family is what I'll do," growled George. He stood up and shook his fist. His eyes became distant, and he began to wobble.

"Dad, are you all right?"

George grabbed his chest and gasped for air.

Savannah reached for her cellphone again. "I'm calling 911. I think he's having a heart attack."

All down the street, windows lit up when the medics pushed George on a stretcher through the wintry night air and placed him in the back of the ambulance.

"I'm sure I'll be fine here by myself," Savannah assured her mother, feeling as though she was trapped in a nightmare. "I wish I could go with you to the hospital, but I need to stay here in case—" She couldn't bring herself to mention her son's disappearance; her nerves were more on edge than ever. After the ambulance drove off with her parents, Savannah turned to go back into the house. She paused when she saw the Santa sculpture that Noel had helped wrap the red-and-white lights around. Somebody had knocked it to the ground. Probably Scotty in his rage. She tried to make it stand back up, so it would help Noel find his house when he returned, but the wire supports had broken, and it kept flopping back over. Savannah collapsed over the lights and wept.

"Mrs. Graysen," said a child's soft voice, somewhere to her left.

Savannah looked up and saw Stacy standing in the

dark, wrapped in a black blanket with white spiders stitched all over it. His face bare of makeup still appeared feminine, prettier than Savannah had ever been as a child.

"Stacy." Savannah wiped her eyes on her arm. "Are you sure you haven't seen Noel?"

"No," he said, shaking his head. "But I heard the AMBER Alert and all. And I just want to say, um, I hope Noel is okay. If you need anything, all you have to do is ask me."

Savannah convulsed, trying to fight back the tears. "Thank you, Stacy." She tried to offer Stacy a smile but feared she looked like a gargoyle instead. "Thank you."

CHAPTER THIRTEEN

Savannah was so exhausted by 10 AM, she could stay awake no longer and nodded off. She almost didn't hear her cellphone but managed to answer it before it went into voicemail.

"You fat little bitch!" Scotty growled through the phone. "I don't know what you're up to, sending the cops to find me at my sister's place, trying to make it look like I kidnapped Noel."

"It sure took you long enough to return my call," said Savannah. "You can hate me all you want, but you're obviously more worried about your reputation than you are about Noel."

"Because I don't believe a damn word of it, you ass-ugly pig. You're hiding Noel somewhere, doing all of this to get back at me. What've you been telling the police that I did to Noel?"

"I'm hanging up now," said Savannah, shaking. "All

of this has caused my father to have a heart attack. I haven't had a minute's sleep, waiting for news on him or our missing son. If you have an ounce of love left for Noel, you'll do everything you can to find him, otherwise don't ever contact me again."

Savannah lowered her phone after ending the call. Was this what Scotty had thought of her the whole time? All of their years of marriage and lovemaking? Had fifteen pounds and a few wrinkles turned her into a disgusting pig? It seemed so evil the things coming from his mouth— the man she thought she knew better than she knew herself.

She looked through every window in her house for the hundredth time, hoping to see Noel coming home. Every scream of children playing in the neighborhood, every rattle of the mailbox, every car door slamming, every engine revving, every boom from a passing car stereo snapped her to attention, ending in false hopes every time.

And then there were the door knocks from at least three or four different neighbors, bragging about hearing of the AMBER Alert for Noel. The community darlings seemed more interested in the private details leading to her son's disappearance than they were in forming a neighborhood search group.

After two more days of this same hell, Savannah got a call from the hospital that her father had died. The days leading to the funeral were a blur. Scotty didn't dare make an appearance at the visitation or graveside. A police officer had volunteered to stay at Savannah's house while she attended the funeral. This gave Savannah peace of mind because she was still holding out in faith that Noel had just become lost and would find his way home.

The afternoon sun was just beginning to warm the air when she pulled into her driveway with her mother, who chose to remain at Savannah's side. A second police car was in her driveway. The taller officer she had spoken with the most during the investigation stepped out of the car. He was holding a yellow folder.

"It's the chief investigator. I think he has some information," said Savannah warily. Her heart felt like it had moved near her throat.

"Sorry about your father, Mrs. Graysen. We finally heard back from Noel's kindergarten and first-grade English teachers."

"Yes," said Savannah, eagerly, while Molly braced her hand on her back.

"They compared the Christmas card Noel drew you with his phonics evaluations," said the taller officer, the chief investigator.

"Were they able to make out what he wrote?" asked Savannah, resisting the urge to grab the report from the officer's hand.

"We have to keep the card as evidence, but we have a copy of the translation of Noel's handwriting according to the combined analysis of his teachers." He pulled out a piece of paper from the folder and looked at it grimly.

"Basically, both teachers agreed that this is what Noel wrote. But they ask that you sign an agreement not to hold them liable for any mistranslations as much of this was educated guesses."

"Yes, yes, of course," said Savannah. Without reading the fine print, she signed the agreement with a pen the officer gave her.

"Would you like to read it, or would you prefer me to?" asked the officer.

"Yes, please. I'm afraid I'm too emotional," said Savannah.

The officer held the copy closer to his face and began reading:

"'Mommy and Daddy, I wasn't trying to touch the elf. I was trying to put this card I made for you in the elf's hands like my birthday card he was holding. I think I caused the elf to get hurt real bad and made Daddy go away.'"

"Noel must have found the elf in the garbage and didn't know Scotty had smashed its face. It's my fault, I warned Noel not to touch the elf until after Christmas, or it might get sick." Savannah looked up at the clouds and blinked, trying not to break down again. "I only told him that so Scotty wouldn't see him with the doll and spoil the holidays."

"It's not your fault, dear," said Molly, hugging Savannah.

"There is more, I'm afraid," said the officer, looking back at the paper. "Noel's teachers agreed your son wrote that he was taking the elf to the North Pole so Santa could make everything better."

"That must be why somebody saw him walking down the interstate in the middle of the night, carrying the elf doll," added Molly.

"Have the police not found any clues as to where Noel might be? Nothing?" asked Savannah.

"The North Carolina police might have found something a few hours ago, Mrs. Graysen."

"North Carolina?" said Savannah, grabbing the officer's coat sleeve. "Surely Noel couldn't have walked four states away from here. Do they think it's my Noel? Did somebody find him? Is he okay?"

The officer pulled Savannah's hand away from his arm. "Please try and remain calm, Mrs. Graysen, and we will let you know as soon as we have more information."

Savannah flung her arms in frustration. "Everyone keeps telling me to remain calm," she yelled. "You try remaining calm if your boy is missing, and all you do is wait and wait day after day. I've already been to one funeral; I won't be going to another one, you hear me?" Savannah pointed her shaking finger at the officer before the second officer, who had been watching her home, came between them and pulled Savannah away from the chief investigator.

"My daughter is understandably distraught. We both need to get a little rest," Molly said to the officers.

"There are babies a span long in hell."
—John Calvin

CHAPTER FOURTEEN

Savannah couldn't even talk. The passing trees and buildings all blurred together as she let Molly drive her car to the police station down US 280. She was too nervous even to think, let alone handle the heavy traffic. That morning, the police called her to come to the station to look at photos from a crime scene that took place in Fayetteville, North Carolina. The officer warned Savannah that the pictures were very graphic and involved a boy about Noel's age.

"Try to stay positive until we know anything. Did you take the nerve pills the doctor gave you?" asked Molly, turning the car into the police station.

"I think so. I can't remember," mumbled Savannah, taking deep breaths to calm herself, before stepping into the parking lot in the misty rain.

The chief investigator met them inside and invited them into his office, where he closed the door.

"Mrs. Graysen, I know this must be extremely difficult for you, but we need you to take a look at the photos and see if you think it might be your son." He pulled out a folder from a filing cabinet. "The victim doesn't match any records of any missing children in North Carolina or any of the surrounding states, I'm afraid."

Savannah sat in front of the chief's desk while Molly took a seat beside her. The officer began placing one photo after the other across the desk like playing cards. Savannah forced herself to view them. They were pictures of a nude boy laying on his back in a manger, surrounded by every Christmas-themed yard decoration imaginable; all of them had been toppled over except for the manger and surrounding Nativity scene. The boy's little hands had been tied together with shredded green fabric, and his bruised legs draped over one end of the manger. Somebody had carved the words "Suffer little children" on his chest and stomach. And, just as Noel had, this boy had a reddish-brown birthmark three inches below his left hipbone. The veins in Savannah's neck throbbed. The next photo was a close-up of the boy's face. His eyelashes had matted with dried tears while the head of an elf doll had been shoved in his mouth.

Savannah saw a dark tunnel enclosing around her, and the last thing she remembered hearing was her mother crying out in anguish.

A cold rag dabbed across Savannah's face and revived her sometime later.

"Savannah, honey, you fainted. Here, drink this," said Molly in a broken voice, forcing water from a cup into her daughter's mouth.

Bracing her hands against the desk, Savannah opened her eyes slowly, hoping this had all been a nightmare, but there before her again were the photos of her baby boy, his body on display in the most perverse way. Only death could erase those hellish images from her mind.

"That's Noel. It's him," mumbled Savannah. "Why? Why?" she cried. This couldn't be true, her mind repeated. This couldn't and shouldn't happen to someone as precious and loving as Noel.

The investigator leaned forward, and his forehead wrinkled. "Mrs. Graysen, if you aren't ready to continue this, we can—"

"Oh God, no. I'd rather jump off the Federal Building, but we must keep going; I'm ready for closure." Savannah wondered if it were possible for her to cry another tear. Noel deserved justice. It was the least Savannah could do for him since she was partly responsible for his death. If only she had stood up to Scotty sooner. If only she had let Noel be himself. Molly locked her wrinkled hand on her daughter's hand and sent her strength to continue. Savannah never knew her mother was as strong as she was proving to be. Savannah was only a self-absorbed teen when her brother was killed.

"The green cloth used to bind the boy's hands was a nylon fabric believed to be tights the boy had been wearing. I'm sorry to say your son was the victim of a sexual predator."

"Did they catch him?" asked Molly, while holding Savannah under her arm.

"No, ma'am, but we will," said the investigator,

locking his fingers on the desk, his expression stern. "The owners of the home noticed that somebody had vandalized all of their Christmas props. They had earlier won an award from one of the holiday decorating shows on television, and they found your son early this morning in the manger."

"Who are they? What're their names," asked Savannah.

"The O'dey family," answered the investigator. "Do you know them?"

Savannah took another gulp of water. "No, I've never heard of that name."

The inspector shifted in his chair. "The DNA samples found on your son don't match any of the O'deys."

"That doesn't clear them as suspects, does it?" asked Savannah.

"As a seasoned crime investigator, it seems highly unlikely they had anything to do with your son's death, Mrs. Graysen. They were very distraught at finding your son's body in their front yard."

The officer placed another photograph in front of Savannah.

"Mrs. Graysen, I need you to look closely at this photo. A neighbor's security camera captured what is believed to be the suspect. Of course, it was late at night, and the capture was blurry, but the killer appears to be a man, approximately five-foot-six and slightly overweight. He was captured removing Noel's body from behind the seat of a white truck and placing it in the manger before kicking over much of the family's yard decorations as he could. Apparently, a neighbor's porch light came on, and the suspect high-tailed it out of the neighborhood."

"Do you recognize the man or the truck, Mrs. Graysen?"

"No. It's hard to tell."

"You don't think that man could be your husband. Scotty was driving a white truck the last time we spoke with him."

"No, Scotty owns a car dealership and borrows trucks mostly off the lot whenever he's in the mood. He has his issues, but he would never do—"

"Mrs. Graysen, you do realize you will remain a suspect as long as you keep covering for Scotty? You do realize Scotty has a sister living in Fayetteville, North Carolina, a few miles from the O'dey family, don't you?"

"That has to be a mistake. Scotty's sister lives in Tuscaloosa. He visits her all the time, mostly to spend time with his nephew. Scotty must have another sister he never told me about."

"According to records, he only has one sister, and her name is Sarah," said the investigator.

"Sarah Tatum, yes," said Savannah. "I've known her for years. Well, ever since her son, David, was born. Scotty became like a father figure to him since David's real father wanted nothing to do with them."

"Mrs. Graysen, there is no Sarah Tatum in Tuscaloosa. The woman Scotty's been visiting at 27 North Meadow Divide is named Pam Ragland, and her son is named David Ragland, not David Tatum."

"And this David is ten and loves baseball, correct?"

"Yes. It seems your husband has been covering up an affair by claiming he was visiting his sister and nephew."

"David is Scotty's son?" asked Savannah, in disbelief. But why should she be at this point? It made more sense. David was the son Scotty preferred but not necessarily a child he wanted.

"We would need to get a court order to do a DNA test on David, of course. And, as you know, this could present some issues with him being underage. In the meantime, we're awaiting court approval to access the GPS on Scotty's cellphone and vehicle to see if we can place him at the scene of the crime. We will let you know as soon as we find out anything, including the autopsy report."

Savannah and Molly stood up to leave.

"Oh, and Mrs. Graysen. I would avoid going near your husband in the meantime. He could be dangerous."

"To every thing there is a season, and a time to every purpose under the heaven: … A time to kill, and a time to heal; a time to break down, and a time to build up."
—King Solomon (KJV)

CHAPTER FIFTEEN

Molly had been taking ornaments off the Christmas tree when Savannah came into the living room.

"No, Mother, stop! What are you doing?"

Molly jumped and dropped a glass drummer boy, shattering it. "I'm sorry, honey. I thought, well, I thought seeing the tree and all would be too painful—"

"I want to leave the tree up as long as I can—for Noel."

While Molly began sweeping up the broken glass, Savannah added more water to the base of the blue spruce. They put on their winter coats and headed to Noel's graveside service.

The autopsy report verified that the message from the Bible had been carved on Noel's front torso postmortem with a sharp wooden object and not a knife. Local and national news companies hounded Savannah for an interview. As if there hadn't been enough coverage of the disturbing event already.

Savannah and her mother stood with friends and family in front of the casket while a frigid wind circled them, reminding Savannah of when Noel said it meant Santa was on his way. Scotty had sneaked into the cemetery and stood by himself a few yards away from the guests. He lifted a trembling hand to swipe away his tears and avoided looking at Savannah.

As the grave attendant began lowering the tiny gold casket into the ground, Stacy Beachum, Noel's only friend, moved from between his parents and walked to the edge of the ropes surrounding the casket. He removed a rainbow-colored key from a pocket in his black dress and released it onto the top of the casket.

The guests offered more condolences to Savannah and began exiting the cemetery while Scotty lingered. Savannah clung to her mother as they tried to leave as far away from him as possible.

"Savannah," he yelled, rushing up to her. "Please, let me explain. I need to speak with you."

"Don't come near me," said Savannah, drying her eyes with a handkerchief.

"Is everything okay, Mrs. Graysen?" asked Stacy, approaching Savannah with his parents beside him. Under his black umbrella, he cut his eyes up at Scotty icily.

"What're you doing here, you little freak? Just couldn't stay away from my son, could ya? Admit it, you killed Noel, didn't ya?" growled Scotty. He grabbed Stacy by his neck, breaking his necklace, spilling dozens of little crosses, some of which fell down his dress and others onto the dead damp grass. "Didn't ya?"

"Get your hands off my son," said Stacy's father, Dr. Jonathan Beachum, shoving Scotty's shoulder while a wrinkle formed on his brow behind his eyeglasses.

"You mean your daughter?" hissed Scotty, maintaining his grip.

"If that is what Stacy decides he identifies as, then yes," continued Dr. Beachum. "My child never harmed a hair on Noel's head. I've dealt with worst bigots than you in my counseling sessions."

"Let go of him, Scotty!" yelled Savannah, realizing Scotty was drunk. "Dr. Beachum is right. You're sick, you know it? Sick!"

"I'll tell ya what's sick is calling this thing a 'he.'" Scotty released Stacy, who rubbed his neck and moved behind his parents. They checked to see if Scotty had harmed him.

Scotty sneered at everyone. "Aw, Savannah, I knew you'd go and suck up to that little freak after I told you to keep 'im away from Noel."

"Stacy is a far better person than you'll ever be." Savannah glared back at Scotty. "What a fool I was. Maybe the police are correct in their suspicion of you."

"What are you saying?" Scotty's fists opened palms up, which he lifted pleadingly toward Savannah. "I didn't do anything to Noel, I swear. Look, I should've believed you, okay? I should've believed you the minute you told me he was missing."

"Yeah? Well, tell that to your sister in North Carolina," said Savannah.

Scotty's skin turned pasty. "Oh, hell. The police told you about that, didn't they?"

"How could you lead me on all these years while you were secretly sleeping with another woman? How could you?" Savannah shoved Scotty.

Scotty snarled his lips. "You aren't anything special. I could screw a gangrene knife wound if I have to, woman." He staggered over somebody's grave and then clasped his hands together. "Oh, God. I didn't mean that, Savannah. I swear."

In utter disbelief, Savannah gave one last look at the monster she had married. "Stay away from me, or I'll get a restraining order."

Scotty's expression read defeated when Savannah, Molly, and the Beachum family left him standing alone just yards from Noel's gravestone.

CHAPTER SIXTEEN

A week later, Molly returned home to Egypt, Alabama, and Savannah waited for news about her son's killer. Any news. Her adrenaline picked up when the police chief dropped by unannounced.

"Mrs. Graysen, are you still the bookkeeper for Scotty's car dealership?"

"I haven't even spoken with Scotty since the funeral. I don't imagine I'll ever work for him again. Why?"

"We need to confiscate any records you have on his business. We have reason to believe he switched trucks to throw off a possible investigation, which makes him all the more a suspect in Noel's murder."

"Really? But I thought you said Scotty's DNA didn't match what was found on—you know, at the crime scene." Savannah still couldn't allow herself to visualize any specifics of her baby boy's murder, though the images of the crime photos still tried to eat into her brain like acid. Also, she wanted to believe that everything about Scotty and his life with her hadn't been a deception if only to prove she wasn't delusional.

"Your husband even has an alibi. That still doesn't prove he wasn't involved."

"Oh?" said Savannah, curious to hear Scotty's excuse.

"His mistress claimed he was with her in Tuscaloosa at the time Noel was murdered. But we were never able to test the navigation recorder on the white truck you said he was in that night."

Savannah found herself leaning forward with a creased forehead. "What? Why?"

"Your husband claims that truck got stolen from his dealership after he swapped it for a red truck. But he didn't file a report with the police department."

"What about his phone records?"

The investigator scratched his stubbly cheek wearily. "They don't show him in North Carolina during that time, but he could've swapped phones as well as vehicles."

Savannah led the investigator to the room in her home that they used as an office. The investigator confiscated the computer and file cabinet, which held all the files for Scotty's car dealership.

"Thank you, Mrs. Graysen. I'll keep you informed," the chief investigator said, before Savannah closed the door.

Another week later, Savannah turned on the evening news and jumped up from her recliner when she heard her and Scotty's names, along with video clips from earlier news reports playing across the television screen. She collapsed back in her recliner when she saw the Birmingham police arresting Scotty at his car dealership.

"This afternoon," continued the female news reporter, "Birmingham police found Scotty Graysen's white truck in the woods on land he owns in Tuscaloosa and uses for hunting. According to police, this is a disturbing obstruction of justice. In the meantime, police have shut down access to Graysen's car dealership until they can access the GPS records on every vehicle."

"I didn't kill my son. I didn't do anything to him. These lies are destroying my life and my business," growled Scotty, while officers handcuffed him.

"And what do you say to your wife and concerned citizens about your recently discovered affair and child you've been covering up all these years?" asked a male reporter, holding a microphone toward Scotty's sneering face.

"You're an animal! This is spiritual blackmail," hissed Scotty, spitting at the camera with beady eyes.

"Can you explain what you mean by *spiritual* blackmail?" The reporter extended his microphone from a little farther back this time.

"They know what they've done to me. That's all I gotta say," answered Scotty, before the officer shoved him into a police car and shut the door.

Savannah shuddered. Scotty had seemed to look right at her through the television screen. Did he call the news reporter an animal or her? Here he was playing like some sort of angel. Did he still believe she had accused him of killing Noel? She didn't, of course, but why would he hide his truck at his hunting camp after claiming somebody stole it? Had she been married to a monster the whole time? That could only mean she was a total dimwit and completely out of touch with reality.

As much as she hated to, she knew the neighborhood would appreciate her taking down the Christmas decorations in the front yard. The inside decorations she doubted she could ever bring herself to take down, if only for Noel—his memory.

She put on her coat and went outside. The lighted Santa sculpture was nearly embedded on its side into the grass now. She unplugged it from the extension cord and began unwinding the lights Noel had strung around it while singing his happy Christmas tune before the neighborhood bullies wanted to beat him up. Savannah stopped unwinding. Had one of the boys killed her son? She had informed the police about the incident—about any suspicious person who might have wanted to harm Noel. But had the chief investigator even questioned the boys or their parents about that incident?

When she removed the lights from the broken sculpture, she bent over to place them in a plastic storage container. Something caught her eye a few feet away on the grass: A pair of combat boots. She looked up and almost didn't recognize the next-door neighbors' boy, Stacy. Instead of a dress and makeup, he was wearing torn blue jeans and a brown bomber jacket. His hair was pushed up inside a knit cap. She had never seen him looking so glum.

"Stacy! I didn't recognize you at first. Are you okay? You don't seem yourself."

"I'm not myself, Mrs. Graysen. I may never be myself again." He helped Savannah lift the broken sculpture and carry it to the road, where they placed it beside the garbage can.

"What do you mean?" asked Savannah, though she had her suspicions, given that Stacy was so removed from society.

"I'm tired of having no friends—of everybody thinking I'm a freak. My dad says I'm making a mistake, but he doesn't have to live behind a privacy fence. I want to go back to a real school, have some sort of life, Mrs. Graysen. So, I'm going to look like what the world expects me to look like. Not every kid is going to identify with their birth certificate. Some children are born with both male and female sex organs and brains, you know? But nobody wants to believe God would let that happen, so they don't know or talk about intersex children. They don't know many of them end up killing themselves. The world is only driven to make transgender kids like me miserable."

"You know, you're right. I completely forgot about intersex children. I don't even remember where I heard about it," confessed Savannah, though her insides crawled from discussing such a subject she had been taught to avoid. She didn't want to discourage Stacy, but even if he buzzed all his hair off and wore a man's suit, he would still look and sound like a girl. And he would probably be a victim of a cruel and bigoted society.

Stacy helped Savannah remove the Christmas lights from the hedges under the windows of her home.

"I can't tell you what to do, of course, but I made a terrible mistake when I started listening to my husband and tried to make my son into his ideal of a boy." Savannah took Stacy by the hand. "You owe it to yourself to be happy—to be yourself. The bullies you experience are immature, or they're uneducated. Friends and all of that will come later."

"Thank you, Mrs. Graysen." Stacy's bare lips formed a thin smile. "I wish I could bring Noel back. But I don't believe your husband killed him. A few years before you all moved here, another boy around Noel's age was found dead in a manger."

Savannah dropped the wreath she had taken off the front door. "Here? Are you sure?"

"Mm-hmm," said Stacy. "Kevin De Grasse, a boy from my first-grade class at Susan M. Neeley Elementary School where Noel went. I was in the school Christmas play just like Noel was. The curtains opened, and the audience saw Kevin before we did. He was in the manger, naked."

"De Grasse? Was he related to your music teacher?"

"She was his mom," said Stacy, picking up the dropped wreath. "Wow! I can't believe nobody told you about it. But there you go—just like I was talking about earlier. People are good at blocking out things they aren't comfortable with. If they can't kill it, they pretend it doesn't exist." He placed the wreath in the plastic container and shut the lid.

"Did the police catch who killed Kevin?" asked Savannah, tugging her coat tighter over her chest. She couldn't believe what she was hearing. Never mind her husband's double life; could she not trust the police department either?

With a downcast expression, Stacy shrugged his shoulders and shoved his hands in his pockets. "I don't remember the killer's name, but I remember the police saying they had him locked up and all. They must've thought he learned his lesson and let him out, I guess. I mean, it's not as though he liked to wear dresses or anything." Stacy rolled his eyes.

"Thank you for telling me and for helping with the decorations." Savannah hoisted up the plastic container.

"No problem," said Stacy, turning toward his house.

"One more thing," said Savannah, bringing Stacy to a stop. "You remind me of Noel. I just want you to know he really liked you, and, well, I can see why."

Stacy winked and tapped his fist over his heart twice.

Savannah placed the container in the garage and ran into the house to call the chief investigator. She was desperate to know why he would keep the news of another manger murder victim from her. He answered after the first ring, and Savannah told him everything she had heard but didn't reveal that Stacy had told her.

"I mean, is this true? Do you have the real killer or not?" she asked, realizing her voice had become higher and a touch angry.

After a bit of silence and a long sigh, the investigator cleared his throat. "Mrs. Graysen, I assure you we weren't trying to keep anything from you. We're still looking into the case. We believe Terrance Mangum, the man we arrested, is the man who killed Kevin De Grasse and left his body in the manger. His DNA didn't match that on Noel's body, so it seems to be a clear case of a copycat killer, and the more things like this get publicity, the more it tends to happen. Even if Terrance didn't kill Kevin, he killed two other children that we can prove. When we get more evidence, his case will go back to court. And I regret to tell you, Mrs. Graysen, but it looks as though your husband was seen outside Susan M. Neeley Elementary School in mid-December five years ago when the first manger murder occurred. Do you remember why he would have been at the school around that time?"

Savannah remembered back to the crazy Christmas season when Noel was about to turn two. They had been so busy preparing for the holidays and parties around that time. Then Savannah's father had to have emergency colon surgery, so she had left for her hometown while Scotty stayed home with Noel.

"No. If Scotty told me I'm afraid I don't recall," said Savannah.

"Trust us, Mrs. Graysen. We are working extremely hard on this case, and we'll let you know anything of importance." The investigator ended the call without saying goodbye.

Perhaps Savannah was wearing on their patience, she feared. The last thing she wanted to do was hinder justice for her son.

*"No devoted thing, that a man shall devote unto
the Lord of all that he hath, both of man and beast,
and of the field of his possession, shall be sold or
redeemed ... but shall surely be put to death."*
—Leviticus 27:28 (KJV)

CHAPTER SEVENTEEN

Savannah finished vacuuming up some of the fallen
needles from the Christmas tree. She was tired of waiting
for news from the police department and couldn't endure
being by herself in her empty home. She had never felt so
alone and depressed, even in her awkward, pimpled teens,
when she felt like the ugliest girl in her hometown. Many
nights she had fallen asleep in Noel's bed, and during her
trips to the grocery store, she still bought his favorite cereal
even though there were already two untouched boxes in
the pantry.

She sat at her vanity to begin her morning beauty
routine. Taking a hard look at her reflection, she thought
of the years Scotty was unfaithful to her—off making love
to another woman while she dolled herself up and cooked
him meals in painful high heels. She shoved her makeup
case off the vanity table and, from her hair, ripped the

heated rollers that had burned her fingers and scalp for years.

"I hope you rot in prison, Scotty Graysen!" cried Savannah, collapsing over the table.

After her last tear puddled into the powdery residue of rose blush on the vanity, a strange bit of rebellion seemed to be cracking free from her shell of tradition. The oddest sense of release from years of expectations dared to greet her. She was going to Noel's school and confront her son's music teacher. If Casey De Grasse claimed that Noel was her star student, she should have at least contacted Savannah, especially when both of their boys had been found dead in goddamned mangers, for Heaven's sakes.

Savannah pulled her hair into a ponytail and grabbed her purse. Within minutes she snatched open the glass door to Susan M. Neeley Elementary School. Stunned that not a single security guard had stopped her at the entry to question her visit, she headed down the hall and peeped through the auditorium window. Casey was on the stage, playing the piano, while the students were singing along to words projected on a white screen. Savannah waited until the school bell rang before barging through a sea of students who were heading to their next classes.

Savannah knew Casey had spotted her moving up the center aisle between the rows of seats, but when the woman dodged behind the stage curtain, Savannah called out to her.

"Mrs. De Grasse, please don't run away from me. It is crucial that I speak with you."

"Oh, Mrs. Graysen. Sorry, I didn't—I didn't realize

it was you," laughed Casey, stepping backward two big steps. "I only have a second to prepare for my next class." She came down off the stage using the steps on the right.

"You'll have to forgive me, but I'm still very upset. I mean, why didn't you tell me somebody had murdered your son and left his body on this stage in a manger. You can't tell me what happened to my son and your son are unrelated."

"*Shush* . . . please calm down, Mrs. Graysen." Casey's eyes searched the auditorium to see if anyone had overheard Savannah.

"I can't calm down," huffed Savannah. "Don't you care that the real killer might still be stalking around this school? Or did you just use my son to star in your play then chose to dishonor his memory like this? Hell! Just a word—any word from you could've made a world of difference in those first few weeks after his death."

"Believe me, Mrs. Graysen, I wanted to say something. I really did. I don't expect you to understand this, but I had to—I have to believe the two cases are unrelated. It has to be a copycat murder." Casey licked and bit her bottom lip while her eyebrows curled up closer to the vertical crease forming on her forehead.

"Has there not been any communications between you and the police, for God's sake? Something is going on. Somebody is covering up these two cases." Savannah grabbed Casey's upper arms and shook her.

Casey started weeping. "I have had little communication with the Birmingham PD. Marjorie Beck, with the sheriff's department, handled my son's case five years ago. Look, Mrs. Graysen, all I can tell you is Marjorie was soon replaced and forced to retire."

"Savannah, I need you to take your hands off Casey and leave this school at once," said Principal Harmon walking up the center aisle.

"I'm sorry if I upset you, Mrs. De Grasse," said Savannah, before locking eyes with the principal. "And excuse me for trying to keep the other kids in this school from being killed, Mr. Harmon." Before she forgot it, she reached inside her purse and removed a notepad and pen to jot down the former officer's name with the sheriff's department.

"The children here are perfectly safe, Savannah. I trust you've received the translation of Noel's card from his English teacher."

"Yes, and I meant to thank him," said Savannah, positive she was turning red.

Principal Harmon handed a file folder to Casey, the music teacher.

"Dan cut his Christmas vacation short to help you and the police with that translation. We've done all we can for you, Savannah," he said. "Therefore, I insist that you never bother Casey, or anyone affiliated with this school with matters concerning your son's death."

"Wow. Okay then," mumbled Savannah, breaking eye contact with them both. "Well, thank you all for the massive sacrifice of your time." She pulled her purse straps higher over her shoulder and turned to leave.

"From the latest news reports, it seems your son ran away to escape abuse he was suffering in your home.

Perhaps you should be questioning your husband instead of everyone else. Did you ever think that maybe Scotty wrote that card, pretending he was your son?"

Savannah was so stunned she couldn't think of an excuse or a retort. She tucked her chin and marched out of the auditorium and school.

She had imagined letting Casey have a piece of her mind, but never did she expect to leave her son's school feeling like a beaten puppy who got caught soiling the carpet. It was so easy for the world to go on with their lives, so easy to spout off "thoughts and prayers." But it was hard, unforgivable even, for victims to have to shoulder the blame.

Shutting her car door, she resolved to try to find the ex-officer with the sheriff's department. Since the police had confiscated her computer, she began searching the internet on her cellphone for any Marjorie Becks living in the Birmingham area. There was only one. She called the number, and Marjorie agreed to meet with her for lunch at Alfonso's Big Beautiful Bistro in downtown Birmingham within the next hour. She texted Marjorie a photo of herself so that she could find her in the lunch crowd.

Savannah knew she was probably too early when she requested a table for two with the host at the restaurant. But she didn't want to risk ruining this opportunity. She ordered iced tea and a basket of fresh-baked bread to busy her shaking hands and soothe her queasy stomach. This was her biggest phobia, eating and sitting alone in a restaurant. She felt so self-conscious, as though she was on stage with an audience critiquing her as an unloved wretch. It took everything in her being to order tea instead of a strong cocktail. But she didn't want to make any bad impressions, not now that the world suspected her of being a factor in Noel's death. She could only hope no one recognized her without the usual hair and makeup, though one whole table of women kept looking at her over their skinny shoulders.

Five minutes later, a slightly masculine-looking woman in a flannel shirt and jeans wandered brazenly through the bistro while her gaze alternated between the patrons and a cellphone she was holding. Savannah could easily imagine a pistol strapped to the woman's hip.

"Marjorie?" asked Savannah timidly, when the woman double-checked her phone in front of her table.

"You must be Savannah."

"Yes," she said with relief. "I hope you like bread; I ordered a sampler basket in the meantime."

"I'll just have a beer if that's alright with you?" said Marjorie. She plucked a rolled-up file folder from her back pocket and scooted in the booth chair facing Savannah before propping her elbows on the table.

"Yes, of course," said Savannah, feeling calmer now. This woman was down to earth and seemed on fire to help her for once.

"So, I realized who you were before leaving home. Gee, I'm so sorry about your son and your husband."

"Thank you, Marjorie. I don't think I'll ever be the same. All I can hope for is to get justice for Noel."

"So, ya don't think your husband is responsible, even

after all that came out about him, huh?" Marjorie squinted at Savannah; her chin muscles lifted in a concerned frown.

Savannah shifted her teary gaze toward the ceiling. "I may be the biggest fool in Alabama, but despite it all, I just feel in my gut that the real killer is still out there." Savannah explained how the police and school staff had avoided revealing that there had been a manger murder before Noel.

Savannah gripped the tablecloth. "I'm not accusing the police of being corrupt or anything, but before I turn to the sheriff's department, I thought maybe you could— that you might be able to help me."

Marjorie sniffed loudly, ordered a beer, and quickly looked around the restaurant. Her eyes were moist now. "In case ya didn't know, I'm not with the sheriff's department," she said in a lower, paranoid voice. "They forced me to resign after the police department claimed they had solved the Kevin De Grasse murder case. The boys at my department gave me a retirement party faster than I could turn in my badge."

Savannah's hands began to slide off the tablecloth.

"But isn't this ironic, huh?" Marjorie crinkled her nose with another sniffle before another big swallow of beer. "Here we are five years later, and I wanna tell ya, there hasn't been a day gone by where that damn manger murder hasn't haunted me." She smoothed out the curled file folder against the table near the sweat ring of her beer bottle.

"Are you implying what I think you are? Can I not trust the police or sheriff's department?" asked Savannah, sliding down an inch or so in the booth, ready to lay down and die.

"Look, I didn't say that, okay?" Marjorie leaned forward over the table, forcing Savannah to look in her widened eyes—eyes that now seemed like two crystal balls projecting something fearful, something ominous. "But I will say, before I was forced to retire, my family received threats, so I dropped the case—dropped it."

"And this was after the police claimed to have apprehended the killer, right?"

"You got it, girly," said Marjorie, with another tight-lipped frown. "The torch is in your hands now. These are photocopies of all my research during the De Grasse kid case. Take 'em and let me know if you find anything." She stood up and tossed a wad of cash on the table. "Oh, good luck and be careful," she said before leaving.

Feeling as though she had her fate in the file folder, Savannah shoved it in her purse, not wanting to risk any eyes but hers to see the contents of Marjorie's research. She paid for her tea and bread and headed home as fast as she could without risking a speeding ticket.

CHAPTER EIGHTEEN

The overnight migraine medicine was wearing off, yet Savannah forced herself to take another look at the files she had received from Marjorie. She burned her tongue on her morning cup of coffee as she flipped page after page of photocopies of the crime scene. The only difference in these prints than from her son's murder was the manger was on a stage, and drumsticks instead of an elf doll had been shoved in the De Grasse boy's mouth. The file also included several photos of the Christmas musical being set up and rehearsal images of Casey's son playing the Little Drummer Boy beside the Nativity set in the school play.

She slapped her hands over her forehead and pulled

some of her hair down over her puffy face, in disbelief that she had to relive another innocent child's and parent's worst nightmare. These horrors would never leave her head now.

Flipping another page, hiding the gore of it really, she read Marjorie's notes on the suspect the police department pinned Kevin De Grasse's murder on—a young Black male from Birmingham. According to Marjorie's notes, Terrance Mangum was innocent of this crime for the simple reason that he could not spell worth a damn, and therefore couldn't have carved "Suffer little children" on Kevin's bare torso.

Savannah nearly jumped out of her jeans and t-shirt when somebody pounded on her front door. She gathered all the crime files into the folder and pressed her face against the peephole of the door. Scotty was pacing back and forth across the entry.

Leaving the chain on the door, she eased it open a few inches.

"Oh hell, Savannah, don't tell me you actually think I'm dangerous."

"What are you doing here? I told you, Scotty. I told you I never wanted to see you again." Savannah panted for breath.

"I'm out on bond. But they aren't going to find anything on me. The police checked the navigation records on every car at my dealership, and none of 'em have been to North Carolina. Please, just open the door and let me in. I have a lot that I need to tell you."

"Why were you at Susan M. Neeley Elementary

School the day Kevin De Grasse was killed? The week I was with my father in the hospital."

"Savannah, I swear I don't know where the police came up with that. It was five years ago. Maybe I personally delivered a car to one of the teachers there or something. Hell, if I can remember! Maybe you have it in your bookkeeping records. Maybe you can help me find it."

"I don't have a computer or any records. The police department confiscated everything."

Scotty slammed his hands on the outside doorframe and looked at the doormat. His angry breath left a fog in the late winter air.

"Why did you hide your white truck in the woods, Scotty? Why would you do that?" asked Savannah, keeping her left hand on the door in case she needed to close it fast.

"Jesus, Savannah. I wasn't trying to hide my truck because of what everyone is thinking. After you filed the police report and told me Noel was missing, I was afraid you were out to get me. I was afraid the news media would see my truck parked at Pam's house and uncover that she wasn't my sister, okay? I cheated on you, okay? I cheated and didn't want the entire world knowing, so I parked my truck at my hunting camp, and Pam drove me back to her house in her truck."

"Damn you, Scotty! How am I supposed to believe anything you say? You've been cheating on me our whole marriage. And you lied. You lied to me and to Noel."

Scotty crumpled to the doormat and sobbed in

anguish. Savannah's scalp tingled. She had never seen him show this much emotion, this much sorrow. Tears fell from his cheeks, leaving wet stains on the concrete around the welcome mat. He could hardly speak coherently between gasps for air.

"Ugh, I'm so s-sorry for everything. God, this is killing me," said Scotty.

Savannah pinched her fingers over her tear ducts. This was so raw. So many emotions were returning. She made up her mind that she would let Scotty inside, but first, she ran to the kitchen table and grabbed her cellphone before returning to the door.

"Alright, Scotty, I'm going to let you in, but I'm still hurt, okay? I am going to call Mom, and if you try anything, I am going to scream, and she's going to tell the police. Do we have a deal?"

"Yeah," said Scotty, wiping his face on his shirt sleeve. "I don't blame you if you never trust me again."

Savannah speed-dialed her mother and told her what she was doing, despite Molly's protest.

"I think I can trust him this time," said Savannah, unlatching the chain from the door and moving back several feet.

Scotty stood to his feet and entered the living room. He looked around as if he had missed seeing his former home. His eyes paused on the Christmas tree, and he turned around and wiped his hidden face on his shirt sleeve again.

Savannah thoroughly expected him to scold her for still having the decorations up, but he looked so broken—

like a lost child. She pointed at a chair at the kitchen table and told him to have a seat while she sat in a chair at the other end of the table near the file folder.

"Now, what else did you need to tell me, Scotty?" asked Savannah, gripping her cellphone, after checking to see if her mother was still listening.

Scotty took a deep breath and braced his hand on his forehead. "I know I can never take back everything I said and did. But I don't feel I deserve to lose everything."

"Lose everything?" Savannah laughed bitterly. "You still have your mistress and the son you preferred. Or do you still call him your nephew?"

Scotty squeezed his eyes shut and turned his head. "Pam and I are through, okay? We're done."

"You might as well stay with her because you're never coming back in my life if that's what you're thinking. You don't like being married to fat ugly pigs, remember?"

Biting his lower lip and lowering his head, Scotty stared at the rim of the kitchen table, which he stroked with his fingertips.

"Pam got a restraining order on me. She's got forces in high places helping her. She's suing for total custody of David. All the lies and negative news got to her."

"Surely, Pam still trusts you. I'm sure you never beat David like you did Noel—never threw your hunting buddy around."

Scotty jerked back in his chair as though he had never seen this side of Savannah. He rubbed the razor stubble on his chin. He couldn't even look at her now, and this silence proved to her that she was right. Savannah opened the file folder and grabbed the stack of crime scene images.

"You seem to have a memory problem. I want you to take a hard look at these photos, Scotty. What happened to this boy five years ago wouldn't've happened to Noel if you hadn't crushed his elf and threw it in the garbage—if you hadn't assaulted him on his birthday and threatened never to come home again. And, I don't know, maybe if you hadn't gone to the school the day Kevin was murdered and left in a manger."

One by one, she slid the photos across the table to Scotty.

He recoiled and held out his hands, blocking his eyes from the images. "Oh, God, Savannah! I can't look at this."

"I know, I know; you want to run off to your hunting lodge—your secret life in Tuscaloosa. Well, buddy, you abandoned me here to deal with all of this—these images I'll never be able to forget. You think these photos are bad; the police should've forced you to see your baby boy, naked, raped, and left dead in a manger."

Tears poured down her cheeks, but she didn't crumble. She kept her icy glare at Scotty. "I hate you, and I will never forgive you."

With his elbows on the table, Scotty braced his head in his hands and stared at the images while Savannah tossed a few more photos under his nose.

"Are you sure you don't remember being at the school five years ago?"

Scotty grabbed a photo and sat back upright. "I swear I don't remember being there then, but I remember seeing this boy at the school last December."

"What boy?"

Scotty stabbed his finger on a photo. "This boy here on the stage. It looks like he's tying a sheep to a barn post, there, not far from the manger. I left during Noel's performance to have a smoke, and he was sitting on the steps, smoking. Of course, he was five years older by then, but that's him. I nearly knocked his block off when he said something smart about Noel."

Savannah leaned forward. "What did he say?"

"I can't remember, but I think he was making fun of 'im, calling 'im gay. Then the little shithead took off running. Oh! He said he was the janitor at the school. I do remember that."

"But I swear the police are lying about me being at the school when all of this happened with that other boy." Scotty pushed the stack of photos away. "If I was there, I didn't do anything to anyone. I know you won't ever forgive me, but when I have to go to court, I beg you, don't tell them I hurt Noel. The court and judge will never believe I didn't kill him if you do that."

Savannah took a couple of calming breaths and tried to process such a difficult request.

"You did hurt Noel, Scotty. You destroyed him, in fact. And I hope, someday, you'll let it sink in your brain. I will promise you this: when I see you in court, I will only tell the truth, and that's more than you ever gave me."

Scotty nodded his head in defeat. "Can I just have one last look at Noel's room before I leave?"

"Why? You hated how he decorated his room—made

him pray about it."

"He's still my son." Scotty's face turned purple and lumpy from his anguish.

"All right, but don't you touch a thing. I want it left just like he had it."

Savannah reluctantly agreed and followed a few yards behind her husband, checking one more time to see if her mother was still listening on the other end of the phone.

"I'm still here, honey," said Molly, while Scotty entered Noel's bedroom. "Goodness. I heard everything you two said. But you're about to give me a heart attack, I'll have you know. Get him out of your house and lock the door. I'll keep holding."

Before Savannah could respond, Scotty yelled, "Why, God? Why, damn you?" He stumbled out of the bedroom with his arm over his eyes. He didn't stop until he went outside and slammed his truck door. Savannah locked the door and peeped through the window. Scotty was slumped over his steering wheel and remained in that position before backing slowly out of the driveway.

"Happy shall he be, that taketh and dasheth thy little ones against the stones."
—The Book of Psalms (KJV)

CHAPTER NINETEEN

Wasting no time, Savannah put the photo of the boy, which Scotty had recognized, in her purse and drove to Noel's school before it opened the next morning. She parked and waited for the music teacher to arrive. Within ten minutes, she saw a blue car park, and she knew it was Casey. Savannah jumped out of her car and practically ran up behind the teacher.

"Mrs. De Grasse, I'm sorry to bother you, but I have something I must show you."

Casey picked up her pace toward the school entry. "I don't wish to be bothered."

Savannah grabbed the teacher's shoulder, stopping her. Casey reached in her purse, grabbed a can of pepper spray, and pointed it in her face.

Savannah squinted her eyes, preparing for a blinding blast. "Please don't use that on me. I'm desperate here— desperate, Mrs. De Grasse. Surely you remember what it was like, losing your son."

Casey lowered the spray.

"If you could just look at this photo from five years ago and tell me who this boy is." Savannah pulled the photo from her purse and showed it to Casey, who lowered her eyes to the paper and then staggered slightly, as though she was about to faint.

"He was the son of a man who supplied the live animals and manger for the Christmas musicals at the time."

"Was he there when Noel sang last December?"

"No, he shouldn't have been there. We—I stopped having a Nativity scene after my son was found dead in the manger. And I have caught hell for it ever since."

"But the boy claimed he was working here last December—as the janitor. Perhaps you didn't recognize him after five years."

"Mrs. Graysen, we have a janitor, and unless that boy looks sixty now and has changed his race, sex, and weight, then I would say he was just having a bit of fun with you. But this is not fun for me. I had a terrible nervous breakdown five years ago. I spent a year in a mental institution and was finally able to go on with my life until you started treating me like a suspect—forcing me to relive the hell I went through."

With a scowl, Principal Harmon stomped out of the school, pointing his left arm at Savannah while holding a cellphone in his right hand. "Mrs. Graysen, I told you plainly not to bother our teachers. Now, I'm calling the cops, and they'll make sure you never set foot on this school property again." He lifted the phone to his red ear.

"I'm sorry; it won't happen again," said Savannah. She dashed back to her car and drove off, watching in every direction for flashing blue lights. Three miles away, she began to loosen her grip on the steering wheel. If only she could've found out where the so-called janitor boy lived or at least his name. Finally, turning on her street, a police car sped up from behind and spun sideways near her front bumper, blocking her. Savannah slammed on the brakes, and her heart jumped into her throat. *My God! Was this really necessary?* she wondered.

A police officer with a shaved head and mirrored shades stepped out of his car. He had so many muscles he had difficulty moving. Savannah rolled her window down and leaned her head out of the window.

"You nearly caused me to crash. Is this about Principal Harmon?"

The officer kept his hand on his pistol as though he had no intention of answering questions. "Step out of the vehicle, ma'am."

Savannah opened the door and stood beside her car. The officer reached inside, grabbed Savannah's purse, and began rummaging through it.

"Excuse me, Officer, but don't you need a warrant to go through my things?"

The officer spun around and grabbed Savannah by the back of her neck and slammed her against the side of the car, where he held her in a pinned position.

"I can do whatever I want to murder suspects, ma'am. You open that smart mouth of yours one more time, and I'll get you on a list of charges so long you'll need a fucking telescope to read them all."

The officer released his hold on her and resumed looking through her purse. He pulled out the photo of the boy who claimed he had been the janitor at Noel's school.

"Who gave you this photo?" he asked, holding it near her face.

"I took it myself before my son's school musical," Savannah lied, and she tried to work the cramp out of her neck that the officer had given her. "I was so excited about him being the head elf, I took pictures of everything."

The officer crumpled up the photo and crammed it in his pants pocket. "I'm going to let you go this time, ma'am. But if I were you, I'd mind my own business and take up crocheting or something." He shoved her purse into her hands and returned to his car.

Savannah waited for over five minutes, wanting the officer to leave first. She was shaking so hard she worried she wouldn't be able to finish driving to her home, just a few more houses down the street. Were the police still considering her a suspect, or was this all just some intimidation to keep her from uncovering the real killer? If Savannah didn't move her car off the street, she feared the jerk would get her for illegal parking. Holding her breath, she pulled around him and looked in her rearview mirror. He was now trailing inches from her bumper. She gave a signal and turned into her driveway. The officer paused on the street and watched her as though waiting for her to step out of the car.

Hoping to disprove her fear of this, she acted as though she was on her cellphone until the officer gave up and drove away. Still afraid to get out of the car in case he came back, Savannah called Marjorie to tell her what had happened.

"Hi, Marjorie, this is Savannah—Savannah Graysen. You gave me the files on the De Grasse case."

"Yeah, Savannah, how are ya?"

"Well, I'm a bit shook up at the moment, to be honest," sighed Savannah.

"What's going on? Did you find anything?"

"I believe so," Savannah said, before explaining the whole incident and the photo the police officer kept. "I just wish I could have gotten the boy's name or home address. But there's no way I can risk going back to that school at this point."

"Damn those bastards!" growled Marjorie. Over the phone, Savannah could hear a dog barking and a horse whinnying. "Well then, girly, I think you just got a taste of why I was forced into retirement."

While the street was clear of cops, Savannah quickly climbed out of her car and ran toward her front door.

"I'm in the house now," said Savannah, locking the door. "Do you have any idea who the boy in the photo was?"

"No. Oh, all right, I'll see if I can find anything. But, Savannah, I'm afraid I simply can't get too involved in this again. The torch is in your hands now, remember?"

"Yes. Yes, of course. Thank you," said Savannah, with a bit of disappointment before ending the call.

She headed to the kitchen and made herself a strong Long Island iced tea, and then she plopped down in her white leather recliner and stared at the Christmas tree; many of the needles were fading and turning brown now. Her eyes focused on a glass pig ornament that Noel had picked out for the tree when he was four and loved the children's book "The Three Little Pigs." She was positive the ornament had turned slightly on its weighted branch, or perhaps the alcohol was relaxing her too soon. She began to think of the cops or "pigs," as they're sometimes called.

"But who is the Big Bad Wolf, huh? Who are you?" Savannah found herself yelling in a moment of bitter release.

"Pigs. Pig in a poke. Pigs in a blanket. Pigs in a parlor. Just where would a pig be? On a farm, of course!" she realized, jumping up from her chair. "Somebody with a farm supplied the live animals and Nativity manger for the school Christmas musicals."

Savannah began searching for nearby farms and livestock providers on her cellphone. She called four of the most likely listings, and none of them claimed to rent or donate mangers or livestock for school plays or events.

Maybe the killer is somebody with some sort of Christmas prop business, she wondered. With the religious possibility in the back of her mind, she found a phone listing for Canaan Land Acres.

"'We rent livestock for birthday parties and holiday occasions,'" murmured Savannah, reading the ad out loud: "'Custom-built Nativity props, mangers, and Christian cross adornments for home and yard. We come to you!'" The ad only supplied the name of the business and a phone number.

"You've got to be kidding me. No address? Where's the address?" Savannah called the number.

"Yellow," a man answered after several rings. He let out a long sigh.

"Who is speaking, please?" asked Savannah.

"This here is Canaan Land Acres, ma'am."

"Who is the owner, please?"

"Look, I ain't got time for no telemarketer. Take this number off your list."

"I'm not a telemarketer. I'm calling because I was interested in coming to your farm and see some of your cross designs. Also, I, uh, I know a man who might be interested in renting some of your livestock for a community theater production of Noah's Ark."

"Noah's Ark ya say?" The man's crackly voice perked up. "I think that might work for me. But now, it's like my ad says: I'll hafta come to you. The animals here get too excited when strangers come around."

"Mmph," grunted Savannah. "I always like to see what I'm getting before I—."

"Oh, nothing to worry about there; I'll bring a portfolio of everything I got. And if you see something ya like and you aren't as pleased as David was with Bathsheba, there are no obligations."

"Can you bring the portfolio tomorrow sometime?"

"You name the time, and I'll be there."

"Morning is best for me, say around nine?"

"Nine it is. Now just give me your name and address."

Savannah gave him a fake name but her actual street

address. "I'm afraid I didn't get your name."

". . . Name's Joseph Weeks, ma'am," said the man after an awkward silence.

"For I will pass through the land of Egypt this night, and will smite all the firstborn in the land of Egypt, both man and beast ... I am the LORD."
—God (KJV)

CHAPTER TWENTY

Savannah's nerves had calmed slightly, but only because it was now twenty-six hours after Joseph Weeks from Canaan Land Acres was supposed to be at her home. She tried to call him three times, but he didn't answer or return her calls.

This was just like so many contractors who had stood her up over the recent years, Savannah concluded before burning her fingers on the instant oatmeal lunch she had overcooked in the microwave. What if Joseph didn't call her back because he knew the street address she had given him was Noel's home? Even if Joseph had abducted Noel off the highway, all the news reports on the tragedy would've made it easy to trace where they lived. If that were the case, Joseph must suspect that Savannah or the police might be on to him.

"Oh God!" she gasped, and the veins in her neck throbbed. "What if he tries to escape, or worse, kills as many children as he can because he knows his time might be up?"

After dumping the oatmeal in the trashcan, Savannah dialed the worthless chief investigator and told him about the incident with the aggressive police officer on her street before relaying her suspicions about Joseph Weeks—the creepy manger maker without an address.

"I did not—sir, I did not say the whole police department was corrupt," said Savannah, after the investigator raised his voice at her. "All I'm saying is maybe somebody there—I don't know—your boss perhaps—is protecting the real child killer. Maybe he or they would rather have a go at me instead. And I'm going to go ahead and get this out in the open: I don't care if somebody from your department threatens me—I'm already dead as far as I'm concerned. But my son is going to have justice."

"Mrs. Graysen, I'm trying to help you, but I might have to withdraw from your case if you don't stop these paranoid accusations and let the police do their jobs. Susan M. Neeley Elementary School has suffered enough controversy in the past, and the last thing you or anyone needs to do is frighten the students or community. Besides, as tough as this might be to accept, your son must've had a reason to want to run away from you and Scotty. Perhaps you should examine your spiritual life."

"How dare you twist this around on me!" Savannah screamed. The truth was, not a day had passed since Noel had died that she didn't fight feelings of guilt for contributing to her son's death. She thought of a hundred things she could have done differently. Namely, if she had stood up to Scotty when he first started spanking him over simple things children do. And she should've divorced his homophobic ass when he began shunning Noel and showing a preference for his secret son. She bit her tongue until something wet squirted from her mouth—blood.

"I suggest you watch your tone with me, Mrs. Graysen. Perhaps you should consider taking your case up with the police in Fayetteville, North Carolina, where your son's body was found."

"Hello?" said Savannah, before realizing the officer had ended the call.

She rinsed her mouth in the kitchen sink and grabbed a handful of paper towels to wipe up the splattered blood. This reminded her of the blood she had found on the doorframe on Christmas Eve. Returning to her phone, she dialed Marjorie to tell her about that morning and share her suspicions about the police and Joseph Weeks.

"Those bastards! A woman's intuition should never go underestimated. Apparently, slathering blood on a doorframe was an ancient thing. God commanded people in the Bible to put blood around their doors so He would remember to send the deadly plague to kill the firstborn sons at the other houses. I learned that while on a case years ago. It kept happening in several neighborhoods around Christmastime. But it couldn't be related to your case. Somebody killed your son even with the blood marking on your door."

Savannah began trembling and crammed a kitchen towel over her eyes when her tears began to gush. "But I washed the blood off the door. I, I didn't know."

"Noel's murder is not your fault, Savannah. It's not. Okay, look, I've decided I'm going to try to help you. I should be able to run a trace on Joseph and find out where that farm of his is located. In the meantime, you could be in danger. Stay home and keep your doors locked."

Hymn composed during America's "Great Awakening."

CHAPTER TWENTY-ONE

Canaan Land Acres

A ranch ten miles outside Birmingham, Alabama

Two days earlier

The anointing prickled Joseph Weeks's arms under his long sleeves he wore to cover the wicked flesh as one should. He had a strong hunch the Lord was speaking to him, warning him that part of the business-prospect information he had just written down seemed familiar— "It should be familiar." He tended to get the last few words of the message twice whenever he felt his good master speaking through him.

He left the rustic den of his ranch house and, with guided feet, walked three halls away into his private chapel, which the Lord had instructed him to keep locked as all holy ground should remain. He searched the candlelit walls of the chapel and saw what he was looking for next to the beautiful news articles on Noel Graysen's death: "Santa Needs New Helpers," or rather "Satan Needs New Helpers" as Joseph had corrected in blood ink on the Christmas brochure from Susan M. Neeley Elementary School. Where the brochure listed the cast featuring Noel, he had penciled in the Graysens's home address. The addresses matched.

"Savannah Graysen, you naughty, naughty harlot! The devil hath ensnared your mind to think you could lure a man of God to your house to have him arrested. You should have submitted yourself to your husband as your spiritual leader."

Joseph burst into his son's room at the end of the winding hall. He looked away quickly. His son, Jud, was on the floor at the foot of his bed, pleasuring himself while looking at photos. Jud, now red-faced, snatched his pants up, hiding his wicked nakedness, which was now covered in hair, unlike the boy he remembered twenty years earlier. Joseph stomped into the room and grabbed the photos from his hands. They were photos of the children he and Joseph tried to save—to snatch from Satan's clutches.

"Jud Mason Weeks! No matter what some ensnared preachers tell you, masturbation is a form of homosexuality. You have defiled your holy temple with self-abuse. Be not deceived; abusers of themselves will find themselves in the lake of fire for all eternity!" Joseph grabbed Jud's hair and shoved his face into the floor, where he dropped the photos. "Don't you see? The children of the Great Harlot have tempted you. Satan has made the whole nations of the world to become drunk with the wine of fornication."

Jud looked up at him with a sedate grin and glassy eyes, which deeply troubled Joseph. His boy didn't cry as he used to do when Joseph spared not the rod of God's punishment on him. And Joseph didn't have time to try another exorcism on Jud, not when there were more pressing troubles clawing at the secure gates of their ranch. Besides, the Lord had used the wicked to do his will many times before, and Jud was always eager to help his father punish those who corrupted the will of God.

"But, Father Joseph, you promised you'd provide the twelve disciples and me some concubines to have sex with and expand into tribes. You said we would keep all the virgins for ourselves and kill all the unbelievers—that God would supply 'em like in the Bible."

Joseph looked away. "When the time is right, my Son, God will provide."

"And who gets to check the girls to see if they're virgins, Father? Can I do it?" Jud wiggled his index and middle fingers. "I want seven hundred wives and three hundred sex slaves like God blessed King Solomon with. He liked 'em with towering naked titties—wrote about 'em at least five times in his Songs."

Joseph wondered how much longer he could ignore

Jud's versions of rewards and punishments, not when he seemed to enjoy them more than Joseph intended.

"Son, we must purify ourselves as unto the Lord. Satan is trying to pervert and kill our mission. Now, according to Isaiah 14:21, we must ready ourselves to slaughter the sons for the guilt and sins of their fathers; in case they rise and possess the Earth. Possess the Earth!"

Surely God wouldn't forsake his prophet now. Joseph thought back to when the Lord first called him to be an instrument in this Divine mission to bring the church back to the ways He intended His people to live. And how all of this led up to Noel Graysen and his near salvation at Canaan Land Acres. What a voice Noel had and could've used for the greater good. Jud certainly seemed to enjoy hearing the boy sing; it had such a calming effect on his troubled soul—his deeply troubled soul.

With a bitter snarl on his lips and a lone tear rolling down his pimpled cheek, Joseph took half of the wildflowers he had picked and placed them on Mary's newly dug grave. He then placed the remaining flowers on his son, Mathew's, three-month-old grave. Less than a year earlier, when he was sixteen, and Karlene Mary Polk was only fourteen, Karlene's parents gladly signed consent forms permitting "Mary," as everyone from their childhood church in Athens, Georgia, called her, to wed Joseph. Married at an age that the deceived, new-world Christians would now kill somebody for doing. But from the times of the ancient Israelites under Moses up until the wholesome 1950s, fourteen was considered well ripe for women to be given in marriage to just about any man. And Joseph was thankful he was raised by the original Christians who both knew and preached the truth.

Even Joseph's parents married at the biblical age, the same year the famous rocker Jerry Lee Lewis, nicknamed "The Killer," married his thirteen-year-old cousin.

But like everything else, Joseph came to realize, folks either don't know, or they keep changing everything about the Bible and God's plan for his people, especially pastors who want to keep their massive paychecks.

Unlike the fourteen-year-old Virgin Mary, Mary Weeks was never able to have children. Well, she did but lost the baby because it was born three months premature. This sad event happened after Joseph and Mary's church had made state-wide headlines when they announced that once their baby was born by early December, the couple would play Jesus's parents in their annual Christmas Nativity event.

"It's an abomination right under the nose of God!

Fourteen-year-old children shouldn't be marrying and getting pregnant," said Pastor J.R. Morris to the local news station. Morris had one of the biggest and swankiest churches in Athens, and it was located across the street from Joseph and Mary's church. But any original Christian knew Morris's church, like so many others, was compromising with the world and worshiping at the altar of money, political power, and comforts of the flesh.

The death of baby Mathew Weeks and the negative attention this brought to Joseph's church shut down the planned Christmas Nativity.

"It is God's judgment on perversion," said Pastor Morris and a few other pastors as far away as Atlanta and Savannah, Georgia.

Still suffering from depression from the loss of her baby boy, Mary had refused to leave their tiny starter home, not far from the university in Athens. When she did step out one morning to see the sun, she screamed when she noticed that somebody had spray-painted the words "Pedophiles go to Hell!" across the white wood siding of their home. She was sitting in the driveway in tears when Joseph found her. A few days later, Mary took her own life by sitting in front of a speeding train.

After Joseph stood over Mary's and Mathew's graves and said his goodbyes, he regretted not standing up to Pastor Morris and the other churches. Across the cemetery, the white clouds in front of the setting sun resembled Jesus with outstretched hands. Joseph sensed God was calling him to bring the churches back to the original teachings—whatever it took.

Pastor Morris's congregation was just like all the rest—hypocrites. In their homes and yards, they all have Santa Claus and elf decorations as well as in their books and movies. They pile gifts from Santa under their pagan trees covered in fairy lights and traditional glass witch balls. They hang holly and mistletoe as the Druid magicians did for their pagan ceremonies, and for the whole heathen Winter Solstice, they worship the old immortal wizard, Satan Claws, and his demonic little imps.

They refused to heed the warning in Jeremiah 10: "Learn not the way of the heathen, for the customs of the people are vain: they cut a tree out of the forest and deck it with silver and with gold; they fasten it with nails and with hammers so it won't fall over."

And then the parents "bear false witness against their neighbors" and children by telling them this is where their gifts come from. At the very least, they don't stop other Christians from blaspheming the Word of God by incorporating these myths and evils. Instead, they prefer to blame the nonbelievers for taking Jesus out of the season.

As Joseph left the cemetery, he vowed he would heed the call of God and restore his holy church. And he would never get married again, and thus follow Jesus's instructions to abandon wives, family, and possessions.

By the end of summer, Joseph had sold his house in Athens and had bought a heavy-duty truck. He also purchased a ranch near Birmingham, Alabama, where he planned to live as self-sufficiently as possible.

Several years later, Joseph took over as pastor of a large church in Birmingham but was fired by the congregation after simply reading various Bible scriptures they didn't like. This was a real awakening for Joseph. He began seeing why there were nearly fifty thousand denominations, each preferring only certain Bible verses, and all of them believing theirs was the correct interpretation. Joseph tried to tell the congregation that the Bible warned in the Second Book of Timothy that Christians would get itchy ears and seek preachers who would tell them what they wanted to hear.

After three more failed attempts to start his own church, Joseph had given up on reaching adults and convincing them to get rid of their worldly possessions and pagan traditions. One of his former members wholeheartedly adopted his teachings and started his own Megachurch with its home base in Baton Rouge, Louisiana. But even this pastor had become corrupted by greed and started charging families thousands to "crush their children into true Christians."

Adults were willing to take up their crosses and crucify their bodies up to a point, but they could never surrender their every possession, their televisions, books, and music. They instead embraced easy believism. And the "American dream" gave them their much-preferred prosperity doctrines, G-rated fictions bearing false witness, Super-Bowl-Sunday church services, mansions, blinged-up crotch-grabbing preachers, after-church bikini pool parties, and luxury cars to get them there. They refused to confess their every shortcoming and dirty thought weekly before the congregation, as the Bible commanded. And they just couldn't bring themselves to shun their bosses, friends, and family members who sinned unrepentantly.

"Just as I, the Great I Am, took your firstborn, you must get them as babes, Joseph," God had commanded, His voice as an echoing thunder.

Everywhere around him were lavish displays of lies, blasphemy, and Christian fakers pouring out of steepled amusement parks for Jesus designed to entertain the kiddies while keeping moms and dads comfy in their padded pews and air conditioning. Joseph was going to have to grab servants while they were young, which he did, starting with a boy the Lord instructed Joseph to save on a return visit to Athens, Georgia.

The sleepy Southern town had changed even more in Joseph's absence. The downtown area was now filled with bars and often smelled of urine. Satan had created a breeding ground here and had possessed the lusty college teens with his most clever creations ever: drugs, strange music, and defiant art.

The boy who didn't belong was about four, and already the adults had him marching like a soldier of Satan in a Christmas parade down the street in front of Joseph's old church where he had first met Mary. The small church was now taken over by Mormons, which the true Christians once knew and professed to be a cult until Satan started forcing Christians to become tolerant. Joseph squinted at the defiled building, imagining it burning to the ground as it would have years earlier. But he would be arrested. My how Satan had softened the children of his enemy to be inclusive—to be victims—to forget, he thought, thirstier than ever for vengeance now. Vengeance now.

Joseph felt a warmth travel through his soul—a signal from the Holy Spirit. "You can't let this boy grow up corrupted by lies and wickedness. Snatch him from the pits of Hell," the Spirit whispered in his ear. If, over and over, God commanded and aided His chosen twelve tribes, including the Tribe of Benjamin, to capture concubines to keep as sex slaves, indeed rescuing one boy wouldn't be wrong. Unlike those chosen ones, Joseph reasoned, he wouldn't rape the boy and cut him up into twelve pieces.

Just as God instructed the Tribe of Benjamin, Joseph hid behind the bushes, ready to snatch his dancing prey— his biblical help meet—the Aaron to his Moses. The boy had paused in the back of the parade line to adjust his little Santa boots, which were too big for his feet, and his red-

and-white hat, which kept falling over his eyes. This was a sign. Joseph leaped from the bushes and snatched the boy off the street. He clutched his hand over the boy's mouth as he rushed the lad to his truck parked around the intersection.

"Don't worry," Joseph said to the whimpering boy, while he drove back to his ranch in Alabama, "I'm taking you to meet your Heavenly Father."

Joseph renamed him Jud Mason Weeks in honor of his childhood pastor in Athens and, after a prayerful dedication ceremony, claimed the boy as his son.

CHAPTER TWENTY-TWO

While Jud fed the sheep, donkeys, and other animals scattered in various pens across the ranch, Joseph remained in the kitchen, preparing breakfast for God's higher creation he kept chained up in the barn—eleven male children. He always prepared the boys biblical meals, which he grew and raised on the ranch, including animals with split hooves, figs, grapes, and often cucumbers. And this the boys would eat daily if they had proven themselves worthy unto God. He would never allow them to eat anything that came with a barcode, for this was the Mark of the Beast, which God's holy word warned that no man would eventually be able to buy, sell, or trade without it.

He and Jud needed one more child to have twelve. God always required twelve: twelve tribes, twelve disciples, twelve major constellations, and God gave His people twelve months of the year to provide sacrifices for Him. And they needed to get a twelfth disciple during Twelfthtide, also called the twelve days of Christmas. Joseph had grown to dislike the word "Christmas" because of its commercial takeover and pagan traditions. He would see to it that the world would someday only celebrate the Nativity aspects that were Twelfthtide.

"Father, I found us the last boy!" yelled Jud, bursting through the door with no shirt and his dirty overalls barely covering him. Joseph didn't want to imagine another shortcoming Jud may have had with a child in the barn.

Jud waved a pamphlet in the air. "I've seen 'im, our twelfth. He was rehearsing for the Christmas musical at Susan M. Neeley."

Joseph stopped slicing the unleavened bread and pointed the knife at Jud. "We mustn't select our disciples from that school. The last boy, Kevin, you bumbled his abduction, and now he's dead. His blood calls out from the ground. We need to select our twelfth disciple farther out from the ranch."

"Kevin wasn't the right boy. He wouldn't come with me. He chose to stay with Satan, so I had to—it was an honor killing. You showed me the scriptures in the Bible yourself, Father. You said we could do anything to anyone who rejects the true faith. You said we only had to be nice to the brethren; otherwise, we are casting our pearl to demons, and demons deserve the worst we can give them."

"You were only supposed to kill as a last resort. The police and wicked world don't love and obey God's word, and they will arrest the true followers. I'll not have you exposing our mission." Joseph lifted his hand to strike Jud.

Jud raised his arms to protect his face. "Isaiah 13, Father: 'The Lord Almighty is gathering a fierce army for war—whoever they capture they'll slice open with sharp swords. They'll smash their babies into little pieces; they'll rob their houses and rape their wives.'"

"The females—not the males, boy. Our bodies are much more sacred. Re-read the story of Sodom and Gomorrah—the part where righteous Lot refused to surrender his male guests or even himself to the rapists who were banging on his door. He insisted they rape his daughters instead; the part right before Lot had drunken sex with his little girls." Joseph punched Jud in the arm.

"Is killing less of a worldly crime than raping now, Father?" squeaked Jud, dodging the blows, as tears streamed down his cheeks. "Don't tell me even you've softened to the modern Bible teachings. *'Onward, Christian soldiers, marching as to war.'* Is the Army of God following behind Christ on white horses in the sky on Judgment Day just for appearance's sake—just to sing hymns while Christ does all the slaughtering for them? Why does He call them an army and not his sheep then? Are we just going to blow kisses to all the unbelievers on that great and terrible day?"

Joseph withdrew his hand and stroked his long graying beard. Jud was becoming quite versed in scripture—becoming a better leader of their army of disciples than he had imagined.

With shaking hands, Jud eased the pamphlet up to Joseph. "This new boy wants to be an elf, Father, one of Satan's imps. I saw where he lives. The whole family's big-time blasphemers. They got Satan Claws lit up in devil-red lights in their front yard. The boy's parents even named him Noel; they worship Christmas, Father. He will be perfect for us to save—perfect."

Joseph looked at the pamphlet and his blood heated

with righteous indignation. If only they could save Noel, it would show the world the transformative power of God. Oh, the testimonies he could give. He clasped his hands on Jud's tear-streaked face.

"I've been too hard on you, my son. Just promise me you will continue seeking the Kingdom of God first, and everything else will be added to you."

Grunting and sniffling, Jud dropped on his knees to the terra-cotta tiled floor. "Yes, merciful Father."

Joseph placed the food in a large basket. "Now, go to your prayer closet while I feed the disciples."

A fine mist filled the air that morning, and the dew-dripping weeds slapped against Joseph's legs. He was careful to avoid the fire-ant beds and cow patties while he carried the breakfast basket to the barn in the middle of Canaan Land Acres. He passed by dozens of tall wrought iron crosses he had created and was allowing to rust for customers who preferred a rustic or antiqued patina, while the others he kept from oxidation in a moisture-resistant shed. All the cross designs he had copied from patterns he had seen in various places, but children of the Most High shouldn't own copyrights on sacred objects or Bible verses, but they do—thieves in the temple they were. Joseph couldn't believe that God's words were owned by select people—words necessary to save souls.

He arrived at the barn; the mud-red paint had worn off on half of the towering structure, exposing the gray siding all the way to the central cathedral ceiling. The overhanging trees, now naked of leaves, scratched the rusted tin roof when the wind blew, causing an eerie clawing sound, like the hands of the devil trying to get at God's disciples inside. Satan was the prince and power of the air, after all.

All around the barn's perimeter stood the feeding troughs or mangers as they were called in the ancient world. These, too, Joseph sold and sometimes rented for Nativity props, and he often threw in a bit of hay for the bedding baby Jesus indeed was placed upon by his virgin mother. If only he could carve worth a damn; he would sculpt baby Jesuses to complete the manger nativities.

He placed the basket of food on a worktable and, with a few clanks, slid the heavy iron cross out of the slots that secured the barn door. A rattling of chains deep inside the barn signaled to Joseph that the children were awake and hungry. He grabbed the basket and shut the barn door behind him. Daylight seeped through a few cracks in the wood siding and from four windows, two of which were high up near the cathedral ceiling.

Throughout the barn were wooden cutouts and props Joseph had once used to host the original Hell Night that many churches copied as a substitute for Halloween; only Joseph's version was truer to the Bible. During his short-lived ministerial stint, he knew that it was his Divine calling to scare the children into blessed salvation: Hellish flames; lightning bolts wired with strobes to flash; surround-sound speaker systems blasting human screams and thundering bass; and mannequins wearing crosses and white robes—decapitated victims of the Antichrist, who was sometimes depicted as a Democrat president of the churches' preferences.

What had traumatized the children the most was the locust creatures wearing breastplates of iron in the Book of Revelation. The creatures wore crowns of gold on their long feminine hair as their lionlike teeth protruded from their human faces. Under their thundering wings, their scorpion tails stung actors who had received the Mark of the Beast, a bloody 666 stamped on their foreheads. Other children decided that very minute to dedicate their hearts to God when they saw the robotic dragon standing before a giant beast with ten horns and seven heads as it emerged from a sea of blood under a bloody moon and blackened sun.

But just like Joseph's failed attempts to start a true church, his Hell Nights were banned after Satan lovers decided they were too graphic for the children. Joseph knew it was mostly the product of competing pastors who were jealous of the attendances he was getting at the time, events he had hosted free of charge. One local church's ministry even warned their congregation that if any of its members attended Joseph's Hell Night, they would have no other option but to prevent their children from graduating from their private Christian Academy.

The boys were in their usual corner in front of a row of crucifixes jutting from the dirt. A dozen lifelike sculptures of Jesus dripping blood from His wounds remained there as a reminder of the necessary sacrifices children of the Most High were expected to make to be true disciples.

Joseph lifted the basket toward Heaven.

"Heavenly Father, as you did for Jesus before the

multitude near Bethsaida, we ask that you multiply this food that I have prepared to feed your new disciples."

The amount in the basket never actually increased, but Joseph was convinced doing this would make the food increase in the children's stomachs, as wine turns to blood once swallowed during communion, and the bread turns to the flesh of Christ. Only two boys ever refused to take communion, complaining that cannibalism was illegal. But Joseph showed them the scripture where Jesus said if they didn't eat his body and drink his blood, they would go to Hell.

He placed the basket on another crude dining table and removed eleven plates, which he placed around the perimeter. "When I call your name, please step forward and receive your daily bread. Simon Peter."

The youngest of the boys stepped forward, and Joseph unlocked his shackles, and Simon Peter sat at the far right of the table where Joseph always sat near him at the head. Joseph then called for the boys he renamed Andrew, Big James, Little James, John, Philip, Bartholomew, Thomas, Matthew, Thaddaeus, and lastly, he called for the boy he renamed Simon the Zealot, who was God's most eager disciple.

Joseph divided the food equally among the twelve boys before removing from a bucket eleven metal forks tied to eleven long sticks, which he gave to each of the boys.

After a bit of fumbling with his fork, trying to lift the four-foot-long stick to his mouth, Thaddaeus braced his head in his dirty hands. "I can't eat like this, Father; I'm still starving."

Joseph smirked triumphantly. "And you will starve if you try to feed yourselves. From now on, you will learn to feed one another as the Most High called us to do. I will feed Simon Peter as an example unto you."

After a bit of grumbling, the boys steadied their sticks, trying to copy the feeding moves Joseph had shown them. They stabbed slices of meat on the end of their forks and stretched the sticks across the table, carefully aiming for their brothers' mouths.

"Ow! John keeps stabbing my face with his fork," grumbled Matthew.

"This is stupid. I don't like this food. I wanna go home," cried Thomas. The other boys exchanged sad but frightened glances.

Joseph slammed his fist on the table. "This is your home. You should be thankful I don't make you eat locusts like John the Baptist or starve you for forty days like our Good Lord, who chose to do so to remove temptation. You must learn to take care of your brothers."

Big James threw his fork on the dirt floor. "This isn't our home. You kidnapped us from our real families— families we love. You are trying to make us forget it."

Joseph bolted up from the table, knocking over the wine bottle. "Get thee behind me, Satan! Jesus says in the Gospel of Luke that disciples must hate their families. They must abandon everything to receive eternal life. That makes me your birth father—the only one who genuinely cares about your souls. Do you dare contradict the Word of God?" He pointed his finger at Big James, who lowered his head and slid down in his chair.

"Excellent," said Joseph, sitting back down. "Excellent, because soon the Good Lord is going to provide us with our twelfth disciple, and this shall empower us to become witnesses until the glorious Day of Judgment."

Big James looked up with tears rolling down his face. "But what happened to the other two boys you said were the twelfth? You killed them, didn't you?"

Joseph unhooked a whip, which he kept secured to his belt. "Satan hath ensnared you to sow fear and unbelief amongst the brethren, Big James," he growled. "Those two boys proved to be possessed of the spirit of Judas! Now take off your robe and lean against the whipping post." Joseph pointed to a ten-foot-tall hook-tipped pole sticking out of the middle of the barn floor. He had painted the white pole with stripes of red blood to resemble a candy cane—another new Christian perversion of the biblical shepherd's staff used to keep the flock in line.

Big James removed his robe made from burlap fertilizer bags and braced his hands against the candy cane. The other boys began to cringe as Joseph's whip lashed across his bare backside.

"The Lord is my shepherd; I shall not want. . . . Yea, though I walk through the valley of the shadow of death, I'll fear no—I'll fear no evil: for thou art with me; thy rod and thy staff they comfort me," Big James recited Psalm 23 between gasps of agony until he passed out in the dirt.

"Now," said Joseph, winding up his whip, "it's time

for each of you to do as the Bible commanded and deny yourself and take up your cross daily."

The boys moped over to the row of life-sized crosses and hoisted them out of the holes in the ground and onto their shoulders. Simon Peter got the shortest cross because he was still so small. They began hauling the crosses around the barn, on their "Road to Damascus," as Joseph called it. Along this symbolic road, the boys had to pass in front of Krampus, the pre-Christian inspiration for Santa Claus that many people tried to erase from history for fear of Santa's pagan roots being rediscovered.

To remind the boys of the Christmas wickedness, he had rescued them from, Joseph and Jud had made a replica of the hideous Krampus whose name meant "claw." They used old newspapers and glue to form its goat horns, forked tongue, and hooklike claws down to its cloven hooves. Lastly, Joseph had covered the gross sculpture in dark pelts from animals they had sacrificed according to God's laws.

The heavy crosses, which the boys dragged, triggered a mechanism that made the Santa demon rattle his bells and chains. Krampus Claw allegedly used the chains to beat and kidnap naughty children during Winter Solstice and drag them to Hell for a year, while good children got candy in their shoes.

"He that taketh not his cross, and followeth after me, is not worthy of me. He that findeth his life shall lose it: and he that loseth his life for my sake shall find it," said Joseph. And he knew the boys wouldn't dare try to escape because of the pit bulls guarding the ranch.

CHAPTER TWENTY-THREE

The night of Noel's Christmas play, Joseph kept his truck parked one block from the elementary school. He was always on the lookout for the police and highway patrol for several reasons. At the very least, he and Jud never fastened their seatbelts because it might delay God's plan for them—hinder their blessings and delay the Rapture. Passing out pamphlets with this message, they had caused a temporary anti-seatbelt movement, at least in parts of the South, where they particularly didn't like the government taking away their rights. "Without faith it's impossible to please God," they had printed on the pamphlets. And seatbelts were a contemptuous lack of faith.

"We're close enough, Son. You'll have to walk from here. Kevin De Grasse's mother stopped renting Nativity mangers and livestock from us. I ought to tell the school about her wicked affair with the principal. Women are wicked—they are temptresses. That, my Son, is why true churches, even God, forbid women in the ministry. Don't let the evolved Christians tell you otherwise. Mrs. De Grasse knows we caught her in the office with Principal Harmon; that's why we don't have a pass to wander inside the school now."

"Yeah," said Jud, with his hands deep in his white overalls, looking nervously through the truck's dirty windows. His boots crunched dried mud, bits of gravel, and trash on the floorboard. "She's even more pagan now that we killed her son. Boy, you'd think she would've learned her lesson—learned it big time."

"You killed Kevin," Joseph whispered with a sigh. "And you had better not mess up this *taking* for the Lord."

While Jud lingered on the school grounds, hoping to find the right time to abduct Noel, Joseph kept watch from the truck. He looked up at the cold winter sky, trying to imagine Christ and His Army of faithful saints galloping down to Earth from outer space on their white horses to kill the drunkards, fornicators, thieves, and folks who lusted after other people's possessions. What a shock that foretold event will be to the unbelievers who'll be shooting their guns and nuclear weapons up at the Army, but the wicked and unbelievers won't be able to kill the blood-washed believers in their white robes. Surely Joseph and the twelve disciples he was raising for the Lord would be made high commanders in that Army.

But it seemed only the ancient Christians remembered to include "revilers" in the list of believers doomed for Hell because they didn't love God quite enough to repent. Joseph had to look up the word *revilers* in a dictionary. It seemed everyone reviled or criticized others, especially the modern churches. Surely it was okay to criticize sinners and unbelievers, at least.

An hour later, Jud came running down the street, clutching his baseball cap. Joseph cranked the truck and got chills. Jud was alone; he had failed to capture Noel.

"Don't tell me the boy got away. Did anyone see you?" asked Joseph, speeding down the dark back roads as far from the school as possible.

"I couldn't get close enough to 'im," Jud panted and sniffled. "Noel's dad attacked me, though—when I was smoking on the steps outside."

"Why? What happened?"

"I dunno," giggled Jud. "I told him Noel was one peppy kid. Then I said it's a shame about the stuff they're making Noel do in that Christmas musical—said it goes against everything in the Bible. He got super sensitive about that comment. Even the dad must be a real Santa lover and all."

Joseph was now driving the legal speed on the highway to his ranch. "They don't think that way because Satan has blinded them. They don't see anything wrong with Santa, elves, and all that blasphemy; Noel's father must've thought you were calling his kid a homosexual— the 'effeminate' mentioned in the Bible."

Jud clawed at his knuckles and stared at the white lines whizzing by on the highway. "Give me another chance, and I can get 'im."

"There have been too many mishaps lately. We need

a sign, Son—a strong sign that Noel is the twelfth disciple. I'll make an animal sacrifice to the Lord, and on the night before Christmas Eve, you'll slather the blood on the Graysens' front door post. And if the Graysens don't remove the blood by Christmas morning, we'll know the Lord hasn't chosen Noel to be His disciple—that the Lord has passed over the boy."

Jud's expression drooped. "Okay, Father. But I know Noel is the one. I know it."

The night before Christmas Eve, after Joseph finished the animal sacrifice, a sheep, Jud drove the truck to the Graysens's house and slathered the blood around their front door. He and Joseph returned the following wee hours of Christmas morning when it was still dark. Jud screamed with excitement.

"They washed all the blood off, every bit of it. Noel is the twelfth boy."

Driving down the highway back to the ranch, they

discussed ways to capture Noel without anyone seeing them.

"Noel never plays in his front yard," said Joseph, watching for drunk drivers returning home from holiday parties.

"I bet behind that wood fence in their back yard he does. Rich people like the Graysens; I bet they got the kid all kinds of—wait! Slow down, Father. Is that an elf walking in the middle of the highway up ahead? It is an elf!"

Joseph pressed the brakes, rolling at a crawl a few yards behind a young boy wearing an elf costume.

"It's Noel, Father! Praise God: He hath delivered him straight into our hands." Jud jumped out of the truck and grabbed for Noel, who stumbled face down on the highway while trying to escape.

"Don't!" cried Noel, after Jud picked him up and rushed back to the truck. "Please, I hafta go see Santa at the North Pole. My elf got hurt, and Daddy's m-mad at me and Mommy. He won't come b-back if I don't see Santa. He won't." Noel held up his elf doll and pointed at its crushed face. "Oh, please help me!" his voice squeaked.

Noel drooled on himself. His arms and legs went limp before Jud tossed him in the back seat of the truck cab.

"Shut up! You spoiled baby!" Jud grabbed the elf doll out of Noel's hands and started to fling it into the dead grass on the side of the highway before Joseph reached over and grabbed his arm.

"Let him have the devil doll for now—it'll keep him

quiet until we get him to his—you know." Joseph gave Jud a knowing look.

"Yeah, his new home," giggled Jud, playfully punching his father's left shoulder. He twisted around in his seat to face Noel. "You're never gonna see your evil Mommy and Daddy again. And you're gonna be real sorry you ever liked Santa or wore that demon costume."

In the rearview mirror, Joseph saw the most distressed crease form between Noel's puffy eyes than he had ever seen on a child. With his green-stockinged knees pulled up under his chin, the boy seemed unable to see Joseph or Jud; it was as though he was living in his own lost reality as he sang "The First Noel" in a nervous and whispery voice.

Joseph looked back at the road. They would straighten Noel out soon enough. The boy was truly blessed that they had plucked him from the wicked world. Satan had lost another soul from the eternal fires of damnation, and soon Joseph and His Army of God would begin plucking more souls from the demonic claws of society. It was too late to separate adults from their beloved world but not for the children: "Suffer little children, and forbid them not, to come unto me: for of such is the Kingdom of Heaven."

Bouncing around on his seat with a grin distorting his dirty face, Jud resembled the same child Joseph had snatched off the street in Georgia. Even now, Jud tried playing peek-a-boo with Noel, who huddled behind the seat, whimpering and tugging his elf hat down over his head. Perhaps due to Jud's youthful behavior or because he was his spiritual son, Joseph worried he might have fallen into error by forgiving too many of his shortcomings. He feared that limit would soon break, and Jud might prove a danger to their Heavenly mission. If so, would Joseph be willing to sacrifice his own son like righteous Abraham was?

CHAPTER TWENTY-FOUR

"I just gave Noel his breakfast. The boy appears too ill to eat, but he will eventually. It's time to start deprogramming him. We need to start calling him Matthias, his new disciple name," Joseph said grimly to Jud the following day, as he carried a Christmas present wrapped in all the evil trappings: Santa, flying reindeer, and cute little elves. He sat the gift temporarily on a chest of drawers and fished the Santa Claus suit and white beard out of Jud's cluttered closet.

Jud danced around his bedroom like a monkey, knocking over a crucifix on the wall. "Oh, goodie! Time to de-commemorize 'im. This is my favorite part."

"The word is decommercialize. Remember, my Son, this must be done prayerfully and with pureness of heart. The goal is first to show Noel the error of his ways before he will be ready for the meat of God's word—before he'll be ready to join the other disciples."

"I don't understand, Father. You beat me for lying

about stuff. Why is this okay?"

"I knew we would someday have this conversation. You should be old enough now to understand a lie from a righteous lie. You see, in Romans 3:7, Paul admitted to lying all the time for God's glory. This is why the early church enacted the terms 'Justa Causa' and 'The Righteous Lie.' Saint Jerome knew this and confessed, 'There is nothing so easy as by sheer volubility to deceive a common crowd or an uneducated congregation.' You remember me teaching you about Martin Luther, don't you?"

"Yes. He started the Protestant Reformation, the evangelicals," said Jud.

"Okay, so Martin later added, 'What would it matter, if one would tell a good strong lie for the better and for the sake of the Christian Church?'"

"Yeah, but that's only three church leaders." Jud sneered and carefully pulled on his black mittens.

"Oh, not by miles, Son." He helped Jud finish putting on the Santa costume, along with the most critical surprise underneath it. He turned Jud to face him. "To be a true disciple, you must study the Bible and matters of the church as much as you can. Eusebius said, 'It is an act of virtue to deceive and lie, for the church.' Saint Chrysostom said, 'Do you see the advantage of deceit? For great is the value of deceit.' Saint Augustine, Saint Alfonso, and the best Anglican writers were supporters of the Justa Causa."

"Yeah, but they weren't in the Bible—well, except for Paul," said Jud, checking out his reflection in the mirror behind the door.

Joseph lunged behind Jud, grabbed his shoulders, and shook him. "You fool! I've told you, and I've told you to study God's word; haven't I? HAVEN'T I?" he roared. "RAHAB . . . Rahab lied to protect the spies, and it was counted as a holy deed. JACOB . . . Jacob lied to his father, and God honored the lie as a fulfillment of His Divine plan for Israel. ABRAHAM AND ISAAC, they both lied that their wives were their sisters. Even the Good Lord Himself, who knew the future, told His disciples that He wasn't going to the feast but then went in secret. The righteous lies go on and on." Joseph became short of breath and released Jud.

"So now, my Son," he panted and opened the door, "we, too, can do whatever it takes as long as it's for the Kingdom."

Together they walked prayerfully down the winding dark halls and opened a secret door in the tongue and groove paneling, which led to an unused bedroom where they kept all their freshly captured disciples until they completed the first step in their conversion therapy. Joseph watched behind a two-way observation mirror in an adjoining storage room to monitor Noel's progress and make sure Jud didn't get too carried away.

Noel sat not on the twin bed but in the far corner of the room, with his knees drawn under his chin. The legs of his elf doll stuck out between his stomach and his upper thighs. He stared at the tray of food on the floor by the door. His mouth kept flinching and tightening into a frown. The walls and ceiling had been painted white so the countless scriptures, written in black, would stand out. Printed on the blanket on the bed was an image of Jesus looking toward Heaven with a crown of thorns on his dark-blonde hair and pale forehead.

Jud cracked open the door a few inches and inserted a black mitten inside first.

"HO-HO-HO. I know a little boy who was trying to find me at the North Pole," said Jud, in the deepest Santa voice he could fake.

He stepped fully into the room in his red-and-white fluffiness, holding the beautifully wrapped gift.

Noel wiped his eyes, and his mouth dropped open. "Are y-you the real Santa?" Noel wrinkled his forehead.

"Why, of course, I am, Noel. I'm always here to help one of my best elves."

"Santa! Oh, I knew you would find me. I knew it." Noel jumped up from the corner and ran until he collapsed against Santa's leg and wrapped his arms around Jud's waist. Jud placed his hand behind Noel's shoulder and remained quiet for a minute.

Noel pulled away and held up his doll. "I, um, I accidentally caused my elf to get s-sick and hurt his face; now Daddy doesn't love me and Mommy anymore. You can make everything better again, c-can't you, Santa? I, um, promise I'll never ask for anything ever again."

"Why, of course, I can, Noel, little buddy," laughed Jud in a jolly voice. "Santa can do magic. I have everything you wished for right here in this package just for you." He gave the wrapped gift to Noel. "Merry Christmas, little buddy." Jud snickered.

Noel wiped fresh tears from his eyes on his green sleeve. He snatched off the red ribbon and the separately wrapped lid. A dozen black snakes began spilling out of the package and over the boy's hands. Noel screamed and dropped the gift on the tiled floor. He ran and jumped on top of the bed while Jud cackled with delight.

"Th-that was mean. Why did you scare me?" asked Noel, watching the snakes slither around the room while clutching his elf doll to his heaving chest.

"Because, Noel, Santa Claus is really Satan Claws, the great impostor," growled Jud, removing his mittens and wiggling his fake claws at Noel. "Your parents and everyone lied to you. Satan wants to kill you and send your soul to Hell. Yeah, and every day, ugly demon-elves with razor-sharp pitchforks will stab chunks of your flesh off your body. And they'll crush your bones and teeth into cornmeal and bake it all over the scorching hot flames into muffins and shove them down your throat forever and ever and ever." Jud ripped off his white beard and red hat, revealing the hideous Krampus mask he was wearing underneath.

Noel collapsed on the bed and started rocking back and forth, clutching his elf.

"*Mph*, I want, I wanna go home, please. I, I need my mommy, okaaay?" he sobbed.

Jud scraped his fake claws across the scriptures on the wall. "That won't work. You'll never escape the fires of Hell or be with God or your mommy, no matter how much you cry and ask forgiveness."

Knowing it was his cue to step into the room and

intervene, Joseph barged through the door and thrust a wooden cross at Jud in his Santa costume.

"Satan, I command you to leave this house. This boy, Matthias, has been chosen by God to be His twelfth disciple."

"Argh!" Jud growled. "I will go, but if Matthias doesn't take up his cross and follow God, I will return and possess his very soul! I don't think he'll stop believing in me, the great Satan Claws; even now, the boy clings to that evil elf in his hands."

"The Lord rebuke you, Satan!" hissed Joseph, and Jud backed out of the room, screeching as he had been taught.

When they were alone, Joseph gently reached his hand out to Noel. "Do you renounce Santa, elves, and the way your parents raised you, my child?"

Noel licked his lips, and his chin scrunched worryingly.

"Answer me, Matthias."

"I, I don't know what wenounce means. I'm not Matthias; I'm Noel."

"It's *renounce*, and it means to reject and to hate. And your name is Matthias, my child; you don't have to go to Hell and be tortured by Satan if you will hate your family as the Bible commands you. If you stop loving all the things your parents taught you, especially about Santa and all their other lies about Christmas."

Noel sighed deeply and, as the bridge of his nose creased, his glassy eyes enlarged with distress. He looked around dizzily, as though trying to find an answer or exit from this soul crossroad that every sinner must face.

"But my, uh, mommy loves me, and I love her, too. And my elf didn't do nothing to me." Noel stroked the smashed head under its green felt hat. "He's my friend."

"That elf led you down the highway to Hell. It may look like a doll—a harmless toy—but it is a gateway to Satan. Now I insist you give it to me." Joseph lunged at Noel, but he rolled over on the bed to protect the doll. Joseph grabbed his leg and flung him over, causing Noel to hit his head on the headboard while Joseph wrestled the doll from his arms.

"You will learn, Matthias, that no one else cares for you as we do. And you'll learn to love God and turn your back on the wicked world. And until you do, you will go hungry. Sin and unbelief are to be stamped out by all means necessary." Joseph shook the doll at Noel as he sobbed into the pillow.

"I will make them eat the flesh of their sons and daughters."
—God (KJV)

CHAPTER TWENTY-FIVE

Jud filled the bathtub with warm water and lit a few candles. Back in the hall of the ranch house, he kept passing back and forth in front of the door to the secret bedroom as though something was controlling his legs and his thoughts. A growing obsession he didn't dare speak. He paused and pushed lightly on the hidden door. Obsession was a word Joseph had taught him recently. Jud was sure he now understood when the bad thing was happening to him. Maybe the bad thing would vanish if he didn't admit it out loud.

Satan can't hear thoughts—or can he? he wondered.

He pressed his hands over his ears and shook his head like a dog—a male dog with a female in heat nearby. So unfair to bother the males . . . to make sweet boy dogs restless.

Jud listened through the door yet again. Not good. Noel wasn't singing the hymns from the book Joseph had left him. He was singing a wicked Christmas song.

"Joseph won't be happy. I have to punish the

twelfth—make him good."

Jud licked his lips and rolled his fingers over his thumbs.

Why was the boy so stubborn? Awake or asleep, everything he dreamed about the boy seemed meant to be—"ordained" Father Joseph called it. Jud wanted Noel, or Matthias as he was now called, to be the twelfth. Unlike the other boys, more under his control than ever before. The only problem was, Joseph said Jud had lousy self-control.

Here Noel was, alone, just behind the wall. Jud realized he had his hand under the flap of his overalls, rubbing his penis. Maybe the boy was a Judas—unable to be redeemed—there to cause Jud to stumble and lose his soul to the fires of Hell.

"It's God. Of course, it's God," whispered Jud. He checked through the kitchen window. Joseph was still in the barn, training the other disciples. They would soon be able to leave the ranch on missions and take more children until they could build a kingdom—an army. Everyone would have his own child to teach—to save. Chills of excitement eased his momentary anger at Noel.

"Father Joseph will be impressed with me, and he needs to have fewer burdens. Noel belongs to me instead."

Returning to the hall, Jud spotted Noel's elf doll in the garbage can near the door. Jud would need the doll for his plan.

He felt like a car set on cruise control, like he was six feet above the vehicle and wouldn't be harmed if his body crashed. He opened the door to the secret room.

Noel bolted up from the edge of the bed where he had been sitting. His elf costume was wrinkled heavily in places now.

"Oh, it's you." Noel's chest heaved. "I can go home now, okay? My Mommy, um, she's probably looking for me."

Jud held up Noel's elf doll. "Father Joseph won't let you go home. It's for the best."

Noel ran up to Jud, reached up, and placed his hands on his arm. His face quivered and shriveled into a pre-cry. "Please let me go home. I'm really scared now."

Jud squatted down eye-level and hugged the sobbing boy. "It'll be okay, I promise. Look. You can have your doll back, but first, you have to come with me."

Noel backed against the wall. "You're, um, not going to s-scare me, are you?"

"Of course not. I got the snakes out of your room, didn't I?" Jud smiled goofily, hoping to relax the boy.

Noel bit his lips and looked around as if deciding what to do. "Okay, I guess. Where are we going?"

Jud led Noel into the bathroom and locked the door. "I'm going to baptize you. We all have to wash away our sins before we can become God's disciples."

"What is, um, badtize mean?"

"You have to get in the bathtub, and I'll wash all the evil sins off you so Jesus can save you."

Noel shifted his lips with hesitation. "What did I do bad?"

Jud's muscles began to tense. "You were just born that way—'born Hell-bound through original sin,' Father

Joseph said. Unless you're a homosexual, then you weren't born *that* way. Look, kid, you want your doll back or not?"

"Okay," said Noel. He lifted one green-hosed leg over the edge of the tub.

"No, not like that," huffed Jud. He grabbed his arm and looked back at the door. "Here at Canaan Land, we are like the original Christians. You hafta take off your clothes to get baptized, and somebody else has to wash you. Like Jesus did before he washed his disciples' feet."

"You mean like when I, um, take a bath?" Noel looked up at Jud with wide eyes.

"Completely naked. You don't wanna risk some of your sins getting trapped under your clothes and not getting washed off. That's why we don't believe in sprinkling either. You have to learn these things to be in God's Army."

Noel took off his elf costume with a nervous hum until all that was on him was his reindeer underwear soiled by a urine stain. Jud's heart raced faster when Noel's fingers paused on his waistband.

"I, um, don't want nobody to see meee," Noel squeaked and covered himself.

"I have to. I have to see if you've been circumcised. The Bible says in Acts, 'Unless you get circumcised according to the custom of Moses, God won't save you.'"

"What's circus sized?" asked Noel. The top of his nose creased with concern.

"Father Joseph did it to me the way the Bible commanded. A man of God cuts off the extra skin on your penis and uses his mouth to suck the blood off and clean the wound."

"Jedus wants people to take off their clothes and get saved?"

"Bartimaeus stripped naked to go see Jesus. We all have to. Just be glad you're not Isaiah: God forced him to strip naked and preach butt naked for three whole years. And Saul and his messengers all got naked while preaching for God. St. Francis and Rufino did, too."

"They did?" gasped Noel, before his head tilted sideways with a frown. "Mommy will get mad at me for showing my private parts."

Jud knelt in front of Noel. "Yeah, and you wanna know what's gonna happen to her then?"

Noel's bottom lip protruded.

"God's gonna curse her real bad like He did David's wife in the Bible 'cause she got mad at David for dancing naked for God in front of a whole bunch of people."

"Nuh-uh," said Noel, shaking his head. "I don't believe you."

"What does the Bible say then. Go ahead, smarty, tell me," Jud growled, feeling God's wrath building inside him now.

Noel shrugged his shoulders. "The only story I know is Noah's Ark because he h-has all the animals in the world."

"Yeah, well, Noah's son got mad because Noah got drunk and naked, so the son and his children were cursed into slavery. God even used Noah to help baptize the whole world with a flood, killing babies, animals—everyone."

"That's mean. I don't wanna get badtized." Noel reached for his elf costume.

Jud felt fire from Heaven spread through his body. God plainly showed him that he was looking at a sinner, a tempter, a Judas, whom the world had already corrupted beyond redemption. The only hope left was to perform an exorcism.

"It's okay to punish him," Jud heard the small still voice whisper to him.

"I renounce you, Satan—all your service and all your works." Jud ripped at Noel's underwear, knocking him backward into the bathtub where he held him under, and began washing his sins away.

"Don't hold back; it's not the boy, Matthias, you are punishing; it's Noel, the sin. Get rid of the sin. Get rid of the temptation," the still, small voice whispered again.

At some point through the sloshing water, Jud heard Noel screaming in pain, so he shoved the elf doll in his mouth and continued with his glorious purging. Evil elf imps had possessed Noel, making him refuse to sing the traditional hymns. His preference for the Santa songs needed to be silenced.

Fleshly visions kept invading Jud's mind along with the spankings and beatings he had received as a little boy from Father Joseph. The best were his memories in his red-and-white costume in the Santa Shack out behind the barn. Those exciting moments when Joseph would let Jud punish the other boys—punish them however he wanted—as a last resort. With time, Jud was sure the boys had it figured out that he was the Santa in the Shack. "Ho-

Ho-Ho! Do you want to sit on Santa's lap next Christmas, kiddies?" The ones who had resisted the hardest now only looked at him with cold, angry eyes; the others never looked at him. The important thing—the thing Father Joseph wanted—was they all learned how evil Santa was. After a biblical education on the danger of eternal Hell, they were undoubtedly grateful for the lesson. Jud wondered if any of them secretly relished the memories as he still did—their stunned heated faces, their tears, the—

Jud's thoughts were going too dark now, so he did as Father Joseph had taught him in times of lust, and he forced his mind on the Holy Spirit overshadowing little Virgin Mary, impregnating her—a beautiful thing. Always let your body be possessed by the Spirit. This brought the most satisfying release, not just for the sinners but for Jud, as well. Besides, if you reject the Holy Spirit, there is no more sacrifice for sin left. Only Hell awaited.

He jumped out of the water and pulled up his overalls after Father Joseph kicked in the door to the bathroom.

Joseph's face turned ashen, and his horrified gaze moved from Jud's waist to Noel's lifeless body lying face down over the side of the tub.

"Jud Mason Weeks, what have you done?" yelled Joseph. He dropped to his knees and checked Noel's pulse. "You killed him. You killed Matthias."

The nervous tick in Jud's neck returned. "He refused to get baptized—said God was mean and wouldn't stop singing songs about Satan Claws. He turned into another Judas, Father, another Judas. You said, Father—you said we, too, can do whatever it takes as long as it's for the

Kingdom. Remember the scripture in Luke 19 when Jesus said to kill people who don't want him to be their king—he said to kill them now, Father."

He knelt over in front of Joseph and sobbed. "If I'm—if I'm not all that you made me, then please don't beat me anymore, just kill me—sacrifice me to God." Jud wanted to die now more than ever; he didn't know why he had killed sweet, beautiful Noel. Something was wrong with him. He had been careful to avoid the temptation of girls—the lesser Adams—the "lesser of God's likeness." Father Joseph had to be right; the Devil was trying to destroy Jud's higher calling, his ministry.

After a few moments of what appeared like guilty reflection, as though he wanted to confess something to Jud, Joseph nodded softly. "You had better make the sacrifice of Matthias count then, boy. Take him as far from the ranch as possible. As a reminder that the birth of Jesus is the reason for the season. Put Matthias's body on display at a place where the blasphemy is glaring."

"I know . . . I'll dump his body at one of those houses that's all lit up like Sin City—those houses that win the Christmas decorating contests," said Jud, searching his father's face for just one sign of his pleasure, an excited pleasure he barely remembered causing him. Jud longed for those moments of his childhood when his father held him so close, flesh to flesh, when Joseph had stroked his hair and back—a love he never got from the false memories Satan tried to put in his head about having another father and mother. A few deceptive visions of fake parents calling him Daniel on a stage in front of a bunch of people looking up at them. Something about organ music playing made these memories stronger.

"The people didn't learn their lesson the first time," continued Joseph. "They still decorate with their pagan idols, their wreaths and ornaments, and with all their drunken parties and wrapped gifts. 'Thus saith the Lord God: ye have polluted my holy name with your gifts and with your idols.' But did they listen?"

"No, Father. No, they didn't," said Jud with a grin, relieved Joseph didn't beat him for once. Jud sensed a change in Joseph and had never felt so free in all his days. He put his hand on his dad's back, and awkwardly they looked not at Noel's body, or the green tights tied around his wrists, but only at the white tiles on the wall. The condensation trickling down the tiles seemed to form the shape of a bleeding cross.

"They haven't repented because their god is Satan, the god of this world. Time is drawing near. We need to find as many disciples as we can. If God sacrificed his only son, and the people ignore Him, we will sacrifice their sons. Suffer the little children."

*"Let me never fall into the vulgar mistake of dreaming that
I am persecuted whenever I am contradicted."*
—Ralph Waldo Emerson

CHAPTER TWENTY-SIX

Savannah poured the last few ounces of liquor in her glass and considered looking for a part-time job as a bookkeeper. She needed to find a way to keep herself busy, keep her mind off everything that had happened. She had given up on the police; they were not going to do anything to find Noel's killer, and the bastards should just have the courage to admit it. Even Marjorie, who had retired from the sheriff's department, seemed to be avoiding Savannah, and she feared she was on the verge of doing something drastic.

To hell with staying locked inside her home, waiting for the phone to ring. She grabbed her purse, got inside her car, and drove south to Marjorie's house in Homewood, across Red Mountain or Red Ridge as it should've been named. Marjorie's home appeared to be on the most rural spot of land in the quiet suburb of Birmingham. The old Dutch colonial house, open in the front and on the side, had a barn surrounded by a ranch-style fence. A small pine forest encroached on the back and left side of the property.

Savannah parked in the driveway and rang the doorbell. After what seemed like three minutes, she banged on the door.

"Marjorie, it's Savannah Graysen. Please come to the door; I'm getting concerned. You said you would get back to me."

She looked through the beveled-glass window in the door and saw a distant shadow scurry through a lit doorway. Somebody turned out a light in that area. After another three minutes, Savannah felt her heart sink. What had made Marjorie decide to turn her back on her? What could she possibly do now? Her last hope seemed to have slammed a door in her face. Or perhaps something had happened to Marjorie. Maybe somebody from the sheriff's department was in her house and had done something to Marjorie. Either way, she wasn't about to drive back home without getting some sort of answer.

Walking back to her car at a casual speed, Savannah concocted a plan. She would pretend to drive away, park her car off the road, and sneak back to the property.

Within minutes she had done that very thing. She cut through the trees on the left side of the house and opened a wooden gate at the back. Around the red-tip photinia bushes, screening the back patio, she saw a woman, a little younger than Marjorie, with a blonde ponytail, and she was grilling something on a cooker.

"Damn, damn, damn! I must have come to the wrong house," Savannah said under her breath. But she knew it was the address in the phone listing for Marjorie. She turned to leave, and an Australian Shepherd came around the hedges and barked at her. Then around the bushes, the blonde woman appeared, holding a pistol.

"You had better have a great excuse to be snooping around on this property." She cocked the pistol and aimed it at her.

"Please don't shoot. I'm Savannah Graysen. Marjorie is working on a case for me. I thought something might have happened to her considering her problems with the police and all. I must have come to the wrong house. I'm so sorry."

"Marjorie didn't tell you about me, huh?" asked the woman sucking in her cheeks as her eyes rolled. "I'm T.K.—her girlfriend."

"No," said Savannah. "But to be honest, we haven't had much time to discuss anything but my case. It's, uh, nice to meet you," Savannah lied, trying not to look at the gun.

"She told me about *you*," said T.K., lowering her weapon and calming the dog, which was now wagging its tail. "Anyway, Marjorie can't help you."

"Why? What happened?" Savannah scratched her cheek too hard, causing a sting.

"She's really sorry about it, but she just can't."

Savannah plowed past T.K. and the dog. "Oh no, no, she can't do this to me. My son is dead. She was supposed to trace a suspect for me." In a daze, Savannah climbed a few steps to the brick patio.

T.K. fired the pistol, and Savannah jumped. "Shoot

me if you need to, but I have to talk to Marjorie."

The dog barked furiously as Savannah rushed to the sliding glass doors of the house. She jerked open the door and bumped into Marjorie, who was on her way outside, brandishing a bigger pistol.

"I tried to stop her, Marj. She wouldn't listen," yelled T.K.

Marjorie lowered her pistol and requested her lover do the same. "Shit, Savannah! You're goddamn lucky you still have a head left on your shoulders. We're both expert shooters. I'm a little pissed you trespassed on my property like this."

"I told her you couldn't help her," T.K. said to Marjorie.

Savannah brushed the loose sprigs of hair out of her face. Her hands were still shaking. "I know, I know it was a terrible thing to do. I thought something bad had happened to you. We obviously can't trust the police; you said so yourself. I know you did. You're the only hope I have left, Marjorie. Can you at least tell me why you are dropping me like this? Please."

Perhaps it was to avoid seeing tears moistening Savannah's eyes. Marjorie exhaled and shut her eyes while her girlfriend scooted past them and into the house. "Because, girly, it won't work. It has never worked. As much as I'd love to, this case is too controversial and—"

"And what? What are you trying to tell me? It has something to do with that man who stood me up from Canaan Land Acres, doesn't it?"

Marjorie seemed to be chewing the inside corner of

her mouth. "Trust me. There are reasons cases like this will never get past the law enforcement anywhere, let alone here. Reasons even you don't want to hear because I'm sure you're religious like everyone else in this country. And trust me, I'm not the person to talk to if you're religious." She backed up and reached for the sliding glass door.

Savannah grabbed Marjorie's arms. "No. I mean, I was raised to believe there's a god and all, but I don't think there's a religious bone in my body. Please, this is killing me. I can handle whatever it is you're afraid to tell me."

Marjorie raised one eyebrow with a smirk. "And you have no problems that I'm gay and have a partner?"

Savannah was a tad unused to these situations but was coming to an understanding, an acceptance of nontraditional expressions of sexuality, especially so openly.

"Marjorie, everyone should be entitled to be who they are just like my son should have—unless they're hurting others. And goodness knows I've had enough abuse in my marriage, so I'm not at liberty to judge."

Marjorie sniffled and nodded stiffly. "All right. I'm going to trust you on all of this, Savannah. Come in; this is going to take some time, I'm afraid."

Together they walked through a mudroom, cut through an open kitchen, and into the living area. Marjorie invited Savannah to sit on a sectional couch under the rustic support beams on the ceiling. A chandelier of animal horns and frilly lampshades draped high over a square table with a hand-carved dough bowl and two remote controls in the center. A rustic but comfortable room.

"Would you like a beer or anything to calm your nerves?"

"Oh yes, that would help, I imagine," replied Savannah, wondering what on earth she was about to hear.

Marjorie returned with a heavy-boot swagger, clutching the beers. She pushed the bunched fabric of her jeans down below her knees and fell back in a boxy cowhide chair opposite Savannah. She popped the top off the bottle and tossed it in the dough bowl with all-star precision.

"You cannot reveal this, Mrs. Graysen. You see, before I got axed, I discovered the password to a private database run by the Birmingham Sheriff's Department. Not long after I traced the address of Joseph Weeks at Canaan Land Acres, I did a little more research on him and found quite a bit of information—information that I was so close to getting before they let me go." Marjorie took a few gulps from her beer.

"Don't worry. I obviously can't trust the police either," said Savannah, taking a swig of her own.

"I'm sure you are well aware, Savannah. But there are some really sick religious nuts out there—and they are protected because religion just is these days. Why Americans, in particular, think stories written by ancient Middle-Easterners were actually about themselves is beyond me—Chosen One Syndrome, I call it. They never stop to question why an all-powerful God who can help millionaire quarterbacks score touchdowns—why such a

God always needs chosen people to do all the dirty work. Unless it's bad weather that hits certain cities, then God gets the credit for that. Or if severe weather hits 'good areas,' then they blame gay people like me and T.K. for that, especially if it's a hurricane." Marjorie popped her thumb out of the bottle opening loudly. "See? I warned you I wasn't the person to talk to about these things. You're welcome to leave now if you aren't comfortable."

Savannah was sure this was building up to something dangerous and sticky. "No, please, I want to hear anything you have to say."

"I only have one family member who didn't shun me for being gay: my sister, Megan, a fantastic author. Churches everywhere banned her last book in the stores and libraries because she wrote about a Baptist minister who accepted his gay son. They complained about a sex scene and some language as well. Now here's what I'm trying to get at. Megan dared to point out worse things in their Bibles that Christians want in the hands of every child on this planet. Pure pornographic scriptures about a woman who got horny for her lovers who had penises like donkeys and cum like horses. And her other fantasies about them fondling her young breasts. If that weren't enough, even God, like an abusive boyfriend, said he was jealous of her and would strip her of her clothes and expose her naked body to everyone."

Savannah was sure her complexion was green. "I never heard that one in church, but it has been many years since I attended."

"Ezekiel 23:20. For scriptures like so many of those,

the powers that be tend to keep the archaic wording as a smokescreen to avoid embarrassment. Anyway, you know what all those churches did? They accused my sister of being an atheist and an antichrist—accusations that finished her writing career. But let me tell you, putting those Bibles in every school and hotel is still their number one mission regardless of scriptures so appalling, regardless of the atrocities it has caused and still causes from people who think they are following its teachings."

Marjorie finished her beer and wedged it between the chair cushions. "Corrupt police are one issue, but there is a strange disconnect from logic in this country, a cognitive dissonance, a fascist system that is in place, and there is nothing you can do about it unless you want to be banned and targeted next."

Savannah rolled the sweaty bottle between her hands. "The police I totally get, but I still don't see how the rest has anything to do with my son's murder."

"Trust me, Mrs. Graysen; I cannot pursue this case. If you insist on doing it yourself, you had best be aware of what you may be up against. I am now convinced the police pinned Kevin De Grasse's murder on an innocent Black man. The things I am about to tell you may be why no one wanted to get involved in Kevin's murder or Noel's. They are connected. And there's an even bigger web connecting to those murders."

Savannah gripped her upper chest. Her stomach fluttered, and her air passage seemed to narrow. "Who's responsible? What did you find?"

"Somebody with either the police or sheriff's

department or Canaan Land Acres. I don't know. But it seems like these groups are protecting one another, and I think even bigger protection is coming from the religious protection laws that are gaining far more strongholds on this country than the founders intended. And the well-meaning Christians are either too oppressed, too afraid to go against the flock, or they've become brainwashed."

"Oh, now, Marjorie; I appreciate you trying to help me, but that is very harsh."

"People will silence and despise me more for bringing up religion's dark past, the religious Crusades, Inquisitions, Witch Trials… more than they ever held their brethren accountable for those unimaginably evil actions. It goes back to what I was saying about cognitive dissonance. Even today, those goddamn motherfuckers don't care how many children their priests and members have raped over the centuries."

Savannah's head jerked back, and she had to clear her thoughts over such language.

"Ah-ha! See, there's the brainwashing I was talking about. Admit it, you were more shocked and offended by me cussing than the awful information I told you."

After a cleansing breath, Savannah knew she couldn't deny it. She nodded her head.

"That's because religion trained you only to be offended by certain things. Death and violence mean far less to them than vulgarity or sexual expressions. Mrs. Graysen, do you want to be labeled an enemy of God when these religious groups are protected by the government now—when these groups are the government? If so, then you had better be prepared: there are more and more attempts by religious groups to label atheists or anyone against fascism as terrorists. That is where we are in this world now.

"Whoever killed your son and Kevin and left their bodies in Christmas mangers is trying to send a spiritual message. And I'm afraid it's only going to get worse. You see, Sheriff Johnny-Dale Larson ran for governor of Alabama the year Kevin De Grasse was murdered. One of his campaign slogans was 'Jesus is the only reason for the season.' Old Johnny went so far as to try to make the state remove Santa, Christmas trees and such, and replace these things only with Nativity scenes. And one of his biggest supporters was, guess who?"

"The churches?" asked Savannah.

"Yes, but one in particular. A church ran by Pastor Joseph Weeks, the owner of Canaan Land Acres."

"I see." Savannah was sure her speculations were adding up.

"And guess who I found to be related to old Sheriff Johnny-Dale Larson?"

"Joseph?"

"No, but the two were good friends. The sheriff is a first cousin to Principal Harmon, where your son went to school. Harmon was also a supporter for Cousin Johnny's campaign until he started having an affair with Casey De Grasse."

"She was Noel's music teacher," said Savannah. "Principal Harmon sure seems to have her under his thumb."

"I believe Principal Harmon is afraid. Casey is the daughter of our current governor, meaning Sheriff Johnny-Dale lost to her father, and by Christmas, her son is found murdered in the manger at their school."

Savannah stood up from the couch.

"So," she said with a burst of energy, "the killer is either the jealous losing sheriff or Joseph Weeks, who was known for his failed churches and attempts for a militant Christian takeover of this country. And both are possibly protecting the other."

Savannah paced the floor around the couch. "I can understand why Casey doesn't want mangers in her Christmas musicals after what happened—I'm the same way now. But if Principal Harmon supported the campaign to remove Santa and then changed his mind, why would the police and sheriff still be protecting him and Casey?"

Marjorie scooted to the edge of her chair and folded her right hand over her fist. "I don't think it's so much law enforcement protecting them physically as it is them trying to thwart any investigations that close to home and family. That's why they got rid of me. Principal Harmon and Casey don't want their affair to get out, or they would both lose their jobs. So, everyone is protecting the other. But I'm willing to bet that Casey is feeling like a victim trapped in that web. I think she suspects someone in her circle is dangerous.

"But here is the biggest obstacle of all, Savannah. Joseph Weeks went into hiding, but Principal Harmon and Sheriff Jonny-Dale still have powerful connections to churches in this state as well as conspiracy groups within the national government—all with Christian Dominionist and nationalist agendas. Jonny-Dale received secret information on several police officers and people at the sheriff's department. The man has something over on many law enforcement officers and pastors in the area. He threatened to out me and my girlfriend, especially when I refused to put up with a ton of his abuse and harassments."

Savannah wasn't sure if she had too much alcohol, but she nearly fainted. She sat back down on the couch. "I confess, at first, I was convinced you were either just paranoid, bitter, or over-dramatic. My God! I have obviously been living in a sheltered cocoon all my life." She braced her hands on her cheeks. How would she ever get justice with everything facing her now?

"The easiest suspect to investigate would be Joseph Weeks at Canaan Land Acres then," mumbled Savannah, gazing hopelessly at the dough bowl, where Marjorie had tossed another beer cap.

"Perhaps," said Marjorie, taking a swig of beer. "But I intercepted fingerprint and DNA sample reports taken from Noel and Kevin from the database. Both samples were traced to a boy named Daniel, who went missing during a Christmas parade in Athens, Georgia, about eighteen years ago. What is more interesting is that Daniel is the son of a pastor named J.R. Morris. And I need to show you what I found on that."

Marjorie left the living area and returned with a file folder. She pulled out a couple of pages with photocopies of what appeared to be old newspaper articles, which she handed to Savannah. Her eyes settled on a picture of a four-year-old boy on a church platform. His father was wearing a nice suit and was holding up the boy's hands in a manipulated expression of praise, as if introducing the congregation to the next pastor of the church.

"You mean this is Daniel—the little boy who killed my son?" asked Savannah, reading the article.

"He would be about twenty-two now. Do you think he could be Joseph's son from the original crime scene photos I gave you?" asked Marjorie. "The father and son duo who provided the Nativity props for the school musical."

"I don't know—possibly."

"Well, this is where it looks very possible. You see, I did more background searches on Joseph Weeks. He attended a church right across the street from where Daniel's church was located in Athens. And it seems there were conflicts between the two churches that made the news." Marjorie flipped to the second photocopy with the headline: "TWELFTHTIDE THE NEW YULETIDE?"

"What does this mean, Twelfthtide?" asked Savannah.

"Traditionally, it was a time early Christians observed a series of Christmas rituals starting with a feast of circumcision," said Marjorie. "It lasted from December twenty-fifth until Epiphany, twelve days later. The congregation was forced into extended periods of biblical fasting before the feasts, which is known to play tricks on some people's minds."

T.K. came from of the kitchen, holding a plate of food. "Speaking of fasting, the steaks are getting cold, and I'm going ahead and eating. Anyway, you're wasting your time with Savannah. She's not gonna believe a word of it, or she's gonna use it against us. The younger they get brainwashed, the harder it is to think critically."

"Sweetie, I got this. I'll eat later, thanks." Marjorie motioned for T.K. to leave. She returned the conversation to Savannah:

"During Epiphany, Joseph's family's church got their own epiphany, so to speak, that the modern churches had strayed into paganism and needed a purging before the great Day of Judgment. But what they don't seem to know is the number twelve existed in mythology long before Christianity. The twelve gods on Mount Olympus. The twelve disciples of Mithras. The Twelve Knights of the Round Table under King Author. The twelve ancient Zoroastrian divinities. Even Buddhists with their twelve stages of life. So, when Joseph's church's Twelfthtide movement started shaming the other churches for what they called 'pagan pageantry,' they started gaining popularity. Pastor J.R. Morris's church revolted against them. Morris spoke to reporters and accused Joseph of being a pedophile for marrying an underage girl. The only thing was Joseph was underage as well. He and his teen bride were scheduled to play Mary and Joseph for Twelfthtide. But after the controversy made state-wide headlines, Joseph's church canceled the long event. Mary lost her baby from the stress of it all, and then she committed suicide."

"Right! So, years later, Joseph kidnapped Pastor Morris's son to get revenge," said Savannah, stabbing her finger on the photocopy. "That has to be it, Marjorie. It has to!"

"If that's the case, Daniel is going by the name Jud Mason Weeks now. The past few years, there've been a dozen or more abductions of young boys across the South, especially around Christmas. I believe Joseph is trying to gather Twelfthtide Disciples."

"But why would they rape and kill my boy if they wanted him as a disciple?"

"What you need to understand is you are not up against reason here. If Joseph and Jud are involved in the end-time faction they think God has called them for; you may never be able to get a justifiable answer. They are mentally deranged and extremely dangerous."

"They think God told them to do what they did to my baby?"

"According to the secret database, there was one other child at your son's school who was nearly abducted the Christmas before Kevin De Grasse was killed. The boy's parents filed a report about it, but because of the sensitive nature of the case, the family's name was stricken from the report. The boy was alone in the schoolyard right before rehearsing for the Christmas play. A teenager grabbed him, muttering something about God telling him to take the boy. Apparently, during the struggle, the child's sweater lifted, revealing a bra. Also, a tube of black lipstick fell out, so the abductor thought he had grabbed a girl by mistake, and the boy got away."

Savannah got chill bumps which stung half her body. She was sure the boy had to be Stacy Beachum, Noel's only friend. "Is there any more information on that case?"

Marjorie shook her head. "This is the controversy I warned you about. Many believe God is calling them to take dominion by any means necessary. The others keep quiet because it works ultimately in their favor. They believe only religious people within the same sect—same denomination even—can hear Heavenly instructions. They consider people who've heard voices from the other twenty-five hundred gods in recorded history as schizophrenics or liars."

Marjorie tapped her fingers on the photocopies. "But from the info I've gathered, I'd guess Joseph Weeks and Sheriff Johnny-Dale Larson are part of a diabolical plan to punish the world not just for their corruption of Christmas, but for the whole Bible. They might be holding missing boys captive on Joseph's ranch. If so, they may be severely abused and brainwashed. As far as why they ended up killing Noel and Kevin: people can find a scripture to either justify or condemn almost anything from one book of the Bible to the next. I think the scripture they carved on your son's and Kevin's bodies is proof of my suspicion."

Savannah fanned her face with her hand. "What I still don't see is how you think all the other churches are protecting these monsters."

"I didn't say all churches, Savannah," continued Marjorie. "But what you need to understand is that, even within the same denominations, people disagree about the meaning of scriptures. And if a scripture is too hard to take in an educated society, apologists now call it symbolic or taken out of context. They don't want to admit the Bible has influenced people to do evil things for centuries, so they keep quiet and find something else to blame—video games, acceptance of gay marriage, insanity, porn, Satan."

Marjorie stifled a laugh. "In the Bible, you can't find one example of somebody Satan actually killed. The God they love; however, He seldom spared even unborn babies. God sent a pack of bears to rip children apart because they giggled at a prophet's bald head. But get most any church to see the evil in that, and they'll look at you like *you* are evil or lying. Cognitive dissonance. They need pastors to spoon-feed them the few good scriptures there are or make them see certain evil through rose-tinted glasses. So, they don't want the sins of the church to be uncovered out of embarrassment or fear it will turn everyone against them."

"But not all churches," said Savannah, feeling sorry that Marjorie had become so jaded.

"Oh, come on, guys," said T.K., leaning around the corner to the room. "Most churches would support biblical stoning deaths of people like you and me, Marj, as long as the government or somebody else is doin' the dirty deed. They might not go for stoning disobedient children in the public square anymore, but if a man of God abuses children—a man they've been fed scriptures from for fifty years—well, it's all thoughts and prayers and hush-hush then. Most of 'em secretly wanna take this country back to an old testament theocracy even if they gotta resurrect every fascist dictator to do it."

"Yes," Marjorie nodded a bit wearily. "And that's where pastors with extremist beliefs shared with Joseph Weeks are being sheltered up to the highest courts in the land these days. Many serial killers are religious or think they are prophets—always hearing God's or the Devil's voice telling them things to do, people to kill....

"If any man today tied up his son on an altar and lifted a knife to sacrifice him for God, he'd be locked away, which is what should've happened to Blessed Father Abraham. Imagine a man in this day who'd kill two hundred men, chop off the tips of their penises, and save them in a sack to buy a man's daughter; they'd rightfully be labeled one of the sickest serial killers in history. Not so in the Bible—the churches uphold David, who also killed thousands more, as a man after God's own heart! Humanity has inherited lifetimes of division and suffering from not only justifying Bible events like that but actually teaching them as beautiful things to be emulated! And it's a group such as this, Savannah, that I fear you are up against."

Marjorie closed the folder and handed it to Savannah. "On the back, there is the address for Joseph Weeks at Canaan Land Acres. If I'm right about *any* of this, you'd better get overwhelming evidence, the ACLU—some sort of outside help to prove it, and even if you do, you might be better off moving to Sweden afterward."

Savannah took the folder. "I cannot thank you enough and understand you can't involve yourself any further. I'm going to try to find the killers even if they murder or stone me as well."

CHAPTER TWENTY-SEVEN

Savannah hugged Marjorie and thanked her for her hard work and for supplying her with the research papers. She left through the front door as the noon sun glared through a haze of clouds. When she reached the road where she had parked her car behind the trees, she thought she was hallucinating.

"My car! Where's my car?" she looked up and down the rural road and grew weak in her limbs. There, on the side of the road, where the tires had imprinted into the soft ground, was a wooden cross sticking in the grass with the number twelve engraved in the center.

Savannah took out her cellphone and took a few photos of the cross without touching it. She ran back to Marjorie's front door and pounded on it. T.K. snatched open the door and lowered her pistol.

"Look, Marj has done all she can for you, Mrs. Graysen."

"I know, I know," panted Savannah, before Marjorie appeared over her partner's shoulder. "But somebody stole my car and, and they left this where it was parked. It's a cross with the number twelve." She showed them the photos.

Marjorie and T.K. began cursing and, with pistols at the ready, pushed Savannah to the side as they began patrolling the front yard.

"You go around the back, T.K.," Marjorie whispered. Together they ducked behind hedges and tree trunks, maneuvering between any sizable barricade like war crabs. The dog went with them and sniffed around the edge of the trees.

After what seemed like twenty heart-stopping minutes, they all returned to the front door. Marjorie was holding the cross in her hand, examining it.

"The number twelve in the center is a symbol for Twelfthtide. Here is proof of everything I told you. It's a warning. And let me tell you, girly, soon these crosses will be burning in our yards." With steely eyes, Marjorie shook the cross. "Argh!" she growled, releasing the object, which fell to the ground. "I got a damn splinter." She plucked the shard of wood out of her hand and sucked the drop of blood remaining.

"Shouldn't we have contacted the police before touching that?" asked Savannah, lifting her phone to dial.

Marjorie knocked the phone out of her hand. "Are you nuts? After everything we just discussed?"

Savannah's arms jerked back in shock. "I have to report that my car got stolen at least."

"Oh, hell, no! I warned you, Marj," T.K. kept repeating, walking in circles, chopping at the air with her hands.

Marjorie picked up the cross and shook it at Savannah again. Black soil crumbled off the bottom. "I'm only going to say this one time, Savannah—one time: if the police show up here, they'll know you've been talking to us. They might be after you, but I don't need them or whoever after me anymore. I told you, Savannah. I know I sound heartless, but I told you."

Savannah picked up her phone. "Can I at least have my husband send a loaner car from his dealership? He'll send somebody with a tow truck. I won't tell him about you or our visit."

T.K. and Marjorie exchanged worried looks. "How is she supposed to get home?" asked T.K. "If we take her, they could connect us that way."

Marjorie spat out a stream of cursing through clenched teeth. "Alright, walk as far down the road as you can and call for your tow-truck delivery, but don't tell your husband anything—understand? He's still a suspect."

A quarter mile down the gravel road, Savannah stopped and dialed Scotty. She hoped he would answer because she feared Marjorie would never open her door to her again.

"Oh, Scotty. Thank goodness," she said after he answered. "Some idiot stole my car. I'm sort of stranded. Can you send me a replacement from the dealership? Nothing fancy."

"Stranded? Did you report it to the police?"

"No—"

"Why the hell not, Savannah?"

"I can't, Scotty. I can't trust the police, okay?"

"What are you talking about? Where did you go?" Scotty yelled on the other end.

"I went for a drive—in the country."

"In the country where? Why are you being so secretive?"

"I'm, uh, in Homewood, across Red Mountain." She gave him the street but not the house address she had visited.

"It's the only way I'm going to find out who killed Noel. Please, just send one of the workers from the dealership with a loaner and stop with the interrogations."

With dread, Savannah waited on the side of the road in the weeds until the replacement car arrived. A few miles on the highway heading home, she noticed the same black SUV that had been following her on the backroads. Deciding to test if this were the case, and that she wasn't being paranoid, she made a few detours. She glanced in the rearview mirror. Of course, the SUV brazenly did the same, and there was no one Savannah could call for help. The low fuel light came on.

"Oh, Scotty, why didn't you tell them to fill up the car first?"

The sun was starting to set, and headlights were popping on, blinding her to see much, if any, details of the vehicles around her. She had to go somewhere safe before her car ran out of gas, and she was left at the mercy of the stalker. Her fear turned to rage. She floored the gas pedal and drove right on the gravel shoulder, passing an eighteen-wheeler with "Repent. The end is near!" printed on its back door.

The SUV behind her drove on the shoulder as well, so Savannah pulled back on the road in split-second time to see that the blinded SUV had run out of shoulder and had driven right up the middle of the guardrail. Its four wheels spun a foot off the ground, bringing the stalker to a stop. Savannah kept going until she found a gas station. She pulled beside a pump, turned the engine off, and slumped across the steering wheel.

Her head jerked back to attention when somebody tapped the passenger window with their keys. It was an old man whose beard was down to his chest. Savannah couldn't understand what he was asking, so she rolled down her window a few inches.

"You a'ight, lady?" he asked.

"I think so. Nearly had an accident a few minutes ago. Somebody was chasing me," panted Savannah, pushing her hair from her face.

"You poor, poor thing. Here, let me pump your gas for you."

"Thank you." Savannah gave the man her gas card through the window gap and watched people slopping in and out of the gas station. She hoped the SUV was still trapped on the guardrail. As the man filled up her tank, he whistled a tune that sounded eerily familiar, a hymn, she was sure. She jumped when his white beard pressed against her window.

"Filled ya up properly—twelve gallons. Oh, and make sure you're right with God, lady. It's a wicked world out there. Wicked. Have a blessed evening now." He slipped her card back to her and hobbled to his truck.

When she finally made it home and parked the car in the driveway, her heart resumed a frantic beat. "Onward, Christian Soldiers." That was the song the man had been whistling.

"The sight of hell torments will exalt the happiness of the saints forever. Can the believing father in Heaven be happy with his unbelieving children in Hell? I tell you, yea! Such will be his sense of justice that it will increase rather than diminish his bliss."
—Jonathan Edwards

CHAPTER TWENTY-EIGHT

Despite her doctor's warnings about drinking and neglecting her lupus, Savannah drank herself to sleep in Noel's room. What fleeting comfort it was to imagine him there with her, doing everything Noel loved: giggling, dreaming about Christmas together, talking silly trivia about the boy bands. To have her baby boy there one more time, hug him, watch him sing and dance like his idols. The things she would do differently.

"Oh, Noel, you're so talented. You're going to be a star yourself someday. And Mommy is going to get you a hundred elf dolls—your own little friends—if you want them. And you can play with Stacy. You can play with him every weekend if you want to. We don't care what Daddy thinks, do we? Mommy is never going to let him hurt you ever—"

Savannah woke up, grabbing at her son's favorite Christmas pajamas and his Grinch doll on the bed. But what a cruel intruder time was. Noel's sweet scent was fading fast from his clothes and sheets. Savannah could only pray it was a symptom of her worsening lupus, as her joints and muscles ached terribly when she climbed out of bed.

Her dream reminded her of the police report about Noel's killer trying to abduct Stacy. She scooted in her house slippers to the kitchen and poured any remaining liquor down the kitchen sink. Now was not the time to die. She was going to have to prepare herself every way she could before getting justice for Noel and every other boy and family whose lives had been destroyed. If killing Noel and other innocent children was God's or any religious nut's plan to bring Savannah unto salvation, she'd rather spit in God's face and rot in a burning putrid Hell. At least she would retain every ounce of honest bitterness she rightly felt, retain the hatred toward them that they rightly deserved.

Somehow, Savannah determined while she sipped her morning bone broth and took a hot bath to ease her pains, she had to get as many details about the child abductor from Stacy as she could. But for now, it was time to equip herself. With a peppermint and Epsom salt bath bomb soothing her body, she searched the internet on her cellphone. She needed some reliable body cameras that she could hide in her clothing, somewhere. If Marjorie thought Savannah would need indisputable evidence, she was going to become a walking spy agency. The world would see for themselves that Canaan Land Acres wasn't just some farm that made mangers and crosses or just another religious compound with willing martyrs. They would see it as a wellspring of terrorists. After adding several video cameras and a drone disguised as a bird to her shopping basket, Savannah saw the coolest sunshades with a built-in camera, which would be perfect since she was sensitive to sunlight. The bath bomb had fizzled out, and Savannah wondered if she could order a real bomb on one of her shopping apps, but just the thought of it was too terrifying.

Thirty minutes later, Savannah was sitting in the formal living room of the Beachums' house. A baby grand piano sat perfectly in the recess of a bay window. A pale bluish-green rug, matching chairs, and plush ottoman with floor-length fringe complemented the soft cream-colored walls covered in various molding. Anaya had her housekeeper bring everyone an herbal tea of their choice. Stacy, who was still looking so miserable in traditional male clothing and no makeup, requested violet tea which the housekeeper brought into the lavish room in a whimsical cup that reminded Savannah of Halloween.

"Here you are, Stacy, and in your favorite cup, too."

Stacy's face lit up, but then he lowered his head. "Thanks, but I'd better take tea in a regular cup from now on, Tanja," he said glumly, not crossing his legs as usual but sitting with them as ridiculously wide as the inseam of his jeans and chair arms would let him. "Or maybe I should only drink coffee like other guys. I hate coffee; it tastes like dirt with a piss of burned chocolate."

"Stacy's tutor will be here in an hour," said Anaya in a nervous squeak, while the housekeeper left the room with a slight frown. "What can we do for you, Mrs. Graysen?"

"I'll try not to take long," said Savannah. "And I don't know how to say this exactly, so I hope you will understand that it was only in the interest of finding my son's killer that your names even came up." She rubbed the silky fabric of her chair arm while her cup and saucer rattled slightly from her nerves. Savannah noticed Stacy's slim neck flinch when he swallowed, and his eyes appeared hollower under his mop of dark hair.

Anaya stood up as stiff as a miniature Statue of Liberty. "The police were not supposed to reveal our case to anybody. Confidential," she began rattling off complaints. "You need to leave now, Mrs. Graysen." Anaya pointed to the hall where they had entered from the front door.

"The police didn't reveal anything to me," Savannah half lied, while Stacy's skinny chest pumped visibly.

"Who told you then?" asked Anaya.

"I'm sorry, but I can't reveal that," said Savannah, standing up and placing her teacup on the table near her.

"You are lying. You need to go now." Anaya grabbed Savannah's arm and pulled her toward the hall.

"If you could just tell me what the man looked like. The man who tried to kidnap Stacy. I think I have a picture of him in my purse."

"No. It's too dangerous for Stacy. The police had us sign a confidentiality agreement. We just want to go on with our lives," spat Anaya. "Look, Mrs. Graysen, we are always under attack from religious groups, especially with my husband being a gender psychologist. I tell them even Jesus shook the dust off his sandals and moved on elsewhere when people rejected his message, but these people think they are above Jesus; they intend to take over and make our lives miserable. They don't take up their own crosses and follow Jesus; they put their crosses on other people's shoulders."

"Please." Savannah dug her heels into the carpet. "Please, this could be the man who killed my son."

Stacy jumped up from his chair. "Stop, Mother. I want to look at the photo and see. There's no use pretending. Everybody knows what happened . . . to *me* anyway."

Anaya released her grip on Savannah's arm. "Okay, Mrs. Graysen. But you had better not tell anyone we talked to you about this. The killer might still be out there and come after my child again."

"I promise, Mrs. Beachum. And I suggest you not tell anyone about our meeting either. Especially the police." Savannah opened her purse and removed the extra photocopy of the boy who helped provide the manger and livestock to the school when Kevin De Grasse had been killed. The boy assumed to be named Jud Mason Weeks.

Stacy took the photo and held it close to his face. "Whoever it was that day, he grabbed me from behind. I only saw his face for a few seconds." Stacy's posture shriveled. "He looks like what I pictured—what I *remembered* him looking like—the eyes mainly. They kinda looked too stupid for his age. Kinda like he was a kid in a man's body."

With tears on his cheeks, Stacy handed the photo back to Savannah and hid his face behind his raised arms.

"I, I feel awful. I wanted to say something right after Noel got killed, but they told me to keep quiet since I'm underage. I'm sorry, Mrs. Graysen. I should've died instead of Noel."

Savannah placed her arm on Stacy's back, then went in bravely for a hug. "Hey," she whispered, trying not to choke up. "Hey, sweety, it's not your fault. Please don't ever feel that way."

After a few more seconds, Stacy pulled away from Savannah and continued scratching his left arm near his elbow. "That's part of the reason I carried the icepick to school. I was afraid the man would come back for me again. Two of the kids auditioning for the play saw him grab me. I guess they saw the bra I was wearing and told the whole school about it. I got bullied even worse. They—they called me a freak and said I was the one who tried to abduct the man because nobody wants a queer like me. Some of the boys held me down and pulled down my pants. The whole school laughed when one of them— when he shoved a mop handle inside me. That's when I stabbed him in the leg." Stacy's cheeks turned red, and specks of blood began to surface on his arm, where he continued scratching. "I don't want to ever go back to school even if they let me."

Savannah thought she would collapse from empathy pain for this precious child. She dropped to her aching knees and took Stacy's hands in hers. "Baby, now you listen to me: You don't owe the world any explanations or apologies. If anything, they owe you an apology. But you do owe it to yourself to love and be who you are, and that's a Stacy who's beautiful inside and out. Damn it; if you want tea in a fancy cup, you go ahead and have it with pride."

While Anaya stood to the side, looking so helpless and worn, Stacy buried his face against Savannah's shoulder, and she felt for an odd moment that Noel was the one whose tears had moistened her neck. She stood to her feet and wiped her own tears from her cheeks.

"I promise you one more thing," said Savannah, certain she was exhaling flaming brimstone now. "I'm going to take down these sick bastards, and you won't ever have to worry about them trying to harm or kidnap you ever again. Okay?"

Stacy nodded with a clenched-lip smile that lifted with hope on one side but seemed permanently drooped on the other.

Savannah turned to leave when Stacy fell on the carpet and started convulsing and making gasping sounds. His skinny limbs flapped so violently he looked like he was being electrocuted.

"What's happening, Mrs. Beachum? Is he all right?"

Anaya kicked the ottoman out of the way, knelt on the floor, and loosened Stacy's collar and belt. She then rolled him on his right side. "Get a pillow off the sofa," said Anaya. She took it from Savannah and wedged it under Stacy's neck to keep him from injuring his head.

"He's having a seizure. He got too stressed. I think it's best that you leave," Anaya said, before fluid began to dribble out of Stacy's mouth.

"Are you sure you don't want me to call an ambulance?" Savannah couldn't stand to see the child so helpless. And guilt filled her for causing him stress.

"No. They let children like my Stacy die these days because of the new religious objection laws. Please just leave," Anaya huffed over her shoulder.

"Now therefore kill every male among the little ones, and kill every woman that hath known man by lying with him. But all the women children, that have not known a man by lying with him, keep alive for yourselves."
—Numbers 31 (KJV)

CHAPTER TWENTY-NINE

The cameras and drone had arrived, and Savannah made sure she took time to learn how to use them. She flew the drone in her backyard and watched the video capture on her separate computer monitor, which remained on record mode. The bird drone was totally convincing from the highest point in the sky, but the closer it flew over the ground, it looked suspicious because birds flap their wings occasionally in flight. After she felt that she had mastered using the drone, it was time to take her first drive out to Canaan Land Acres and see what she was up against.

She wore a dark straight-haired wig and her camera shades. She also squeezed into a faux leather dress in black. Savannah had never looked slimmer or so out of character. Perfect. Hopefully, no one would ever guess it was her. As she stepped into her car in the driveway, a child's voice called out, "Wow, Mrs. Graysen."

Savannah looked around and saw Stacy leaning over the top of the privacy fence. He was giving Savannah a thumbs-up of approval. She gave Stacy one in return.

The ranch was located on fifty acres off a rural gravel road in Bessemer, thirty minutes outside Birmingham. There were two other properties on the other side of the road, but their entries were far enough away to give Joseph Weeks the privacy to commit all sorts of crimes, Savannah imagined. She just hoped that they didn't torture her baby too long on this ranch before they killed him. Savannah found it hard to imagine a loving God looking down and allowing or endorsing the torture of any innocent being, especially a child. With the sparkling sun and calm blue skies smiling down on Canaan Land Acres, it sure seemed that way.

The land was enclosed with a ranch-style fence and gated entry. Savannah wasn't foolish enough to think that she could just drive on the property anyway. She parked her car several yards from the gate and released the drone high into the air while she controlled it using her phone app. She kept her eyes on the computer monitor on her dashboard. As soon as the bird drone soared over the fence, Savannah's whole body turned icy. At least four pit bulls were roaming around the ranch.

"Just great," she sighed. "How am I going to get past four drooling jaws of death?" She added an animal tranquilizer gun and darts to her shopping list.

The gravel driveway lined with iron crosses had been laid out in a cross pattern over much of the property. A rustic but sprawling house stood on the back left side. A tall barn and smaller buildings were scattered on the back right side. The front two sections of the cross grid had a massive garden and enclosures full of various livestock. Savannah did a double take at the monitor when she saw a boy running out of a small shed decorated with Santas, candy canes, and reindeer. A sign on the door in red and green letters read "Santa Shack." The boy's little legs could hardly go, and he stumbled over his pants, which were down below his knees. Blood had run from his bare buttocks down to his thighs.

Savannah's heart pounded fast. It was as though she had seen Noel running for his life. She screamed out when somebody tapped on her car window. An older man with a scowl and potbelly displayed a badge against the glass. The little sneak had fooled her with his unmarked truck on the other side of the road. Sweat began to pour down her back and under her arms. She needed to guide the drone—keep it safely airborne—but was afraid the officer would realize what she was up to. Savannah slammed the monitor shut, lowered her phone, and unrolled the window, but all she could think about was the poor boy. *Please let him survive*, her thoughts pleaded.

"This is all private property out here, ma'am. And they don't take kindly to trespassers. I need to see some I.D., please."

The officer examined Savannah as if trying to figure out her blood type. She needed to get out of this situation, or she might never stop the killers. Or she might end up dead herself. She remembered the old-school man-buttering technique she had used to attract Scotty and the backup plan she had memorized just for a sticky moment like this.

"Why, there's no need for that. I'm a sweet home Alabama girl born and bred," cooed Savannah in her purest Southern voice. "I must've taken a wrong turn a while back. You caught me trying to use my digital maps to figure out just where the gee willikers I am. Could you be a dear and tell me how to get to Tanner Farm? You see, I wanted to pick some fresh blueberries for the ladies from my Sunday School class this weekend. And please don't tell my husband I got lost again. He always beats on me and says I don't know my left from my right." Savannah burst into tears, which wasn't hard after seeing the poor boy fleeing from the shack.

"Ma'am—ma'am, now just calm down. To get to Tanner Farm, you need to turn around, go about a mile or so, then turn left on Landdale Road. Then it's three miles on your left."

"Oh, God bless you," said Savannah dabbing her eyes behind her sunshades. "Do you know what I'm gonna do? You know what? I'm going to add you to our ladies' prayer list. There are so many shady characters taking over our good state; they're putting good strong men like you in such harm's way." Savannah fished a pen and pad from her purse. "What is your name, dear?"

"Name's Johnny-Dale Larson, ma'am. And I might just have to come and have me a piece of that pie." He winked over the top of his mirrored sunshades before getting back in his truck.

Savannah waited until the jerk drove off, and then she

tried to get the coordinates of her bird drone on her cell.

The signal was completely dead.

She looked up in the sky just in case, but it was nowhere to be seen.

"The monitor!" Savannah realized. "The recording should still be there."

Her pulse was now one steady sprint. She flipped her monitor back open, hit the play button, and watched everything. The recording was exactly as she had initially seen it. "Yes!" she cried. The camera had captured the boy running out of the Santa Shack. Then she saw what had happened to the bird drone after she had to close the monitor. It had crashed near a cornfield, and one of the dogs had chewed it to pieces. At least she had a bit of evidence they were abusing boys—a bit of gold.

She had been so worried about the drone that the officer's name hadn't crossed her mind until now.

"Oh, my gosh! That was the sheriff Marjorie warned me about."

She remembered that Johnny-Dale was a friend and possible supporter of Ex-Pastor Joseph Weeks. Thank goodness her act had worked on him—this time anyway. Savannah wanted to storm the property now and try to save the poor boy she had just seen, and no telling how many more children, but she was utterly helpless. She was going to have to get the one thing she had fought against ever since her brother's accidental death—a gun—a goddamn gun.

She drove to the safest, most unpopulated location she could think of in Birmingham, a public library, beside an occult shop. There she began searching online listings for local gun dealers. She couldn't believe her eyes, LOADED TO THE GILLS, one of the biggest and best guns and sporting goods stores in the area was owned by a person named Carl Fortenberry. Could it be the same Carl who bullied her in high school?

How many could there be in Birmingham, Alabama?

Savannah touched up her makeup and wig before unbuttoning the top of her black dress. Then she drove to the gun store, watching for any more stalkers. If any car followed her for more than two turns, it was plan over until she could do this discreetly. Hell, Savannah dreaded this so much she felt like she was about to rob a church or something.

She turned off the engine at the guns and sporting goods store and rushed inside with her head down. She had no idea what to look for, so she walked up to the front counter for assistance. She paused in her steps. Sure enough, it was *the* Carl Fortenberry, the Carl Savannah once had a crush on until he crushed her whole teenage years. A kaleidoscope of emotions swirled through her. He wasn't nearly the angel she had remembered in his tight pants. His hair had thinned on top, and everything on him seemed wider except for his shoulders. This was promising. Savannah had grown slimmer with time, but she still needed practice on getting bolder, especially with the tasks ahead. She strutted up to the counter.

"Good afternoon. Can I help you with something?" asked Carl. Savannah relished that his eyes kept lowering to her breasts. He seemed nervous to look into her black shades—shy for once.

She held her fingers apart about seven inches. "I need to purchase a pistol with some potency—one with a sensitive trigger that'll shoot as many bullets as possible."

"Oh," said Carl with a bashful grin. He glanced quickly around, and then his eyebrows lifted, exposing a sparkle in those blue eyes that Savannah remembered him flashing the pretty girls in school. His lips puckered in a subtle look of thirst Savannah had seen on late-night television once, on a man who finally got to see the goods after a long striptease.

Savannah bit her red bottom lip as seductively as possible. "Yeah. I also need a tranquilizer gun and darts, one assassin's knife with a pocket clip, a bulletproof vest, and some bear spray. Do you think you can do that for me?" She leaned over the counter with a little shimmy and lowered her shades half an inch, much more, and he might see the wrinkles in the corners of her eyes.

Carl did a double take and swallowed.

Savannah couldn't believe her behavior, but it seemed to be working. Carl nearly jumped over the counter to start collecting the items. Perhaps she should've gotten bangs and dyed her hair black a long time ago. She tried to think of anything else she might need from this store, as she planned to nerve set foot inside it again. Carl had been in such a hurry he must've strained his ankle as he came limping back to the counter with an armful of items.

"Now we only sell tranquilizer guns and darts. To get the actual tranquilizer, you need to be a state biologist or veterinarian or know one. That stuff is trickier than most people realize. It has to be stored in a cooler, and you have to get the doses exactly right depending on the animal—"

"Oh, I grew up in the country. I know how to knock out a stallion—know how to ride one, too." Savannah bit her bottom lip seductively again.

"Alrighty then." With raised eyebrows, Carl breathed deep and glanced at the weapons he was scanning on the register. Savannah was sure he had missed ringing up an item or two. She noticed a framed photo of Carl posing with his wife and three kids. Savannah was stunned that Carl's wife was bigger than she was when Carl had humiliated her.

"Is that a picture of you and your wife there?" Savannah lowered her shades and glanced behind him.

Carl swallowed hard and blushed. "Oh, that. Yeah, but—"

"She's pretty. I bet you don't need to keep any spare tires for her. I just hope she stays slim; it would be a shame if one of your buddies threw a chicken leg at her or something."

Carl froze for a second, and his forehead wrinkled as though he remembered back to when he had yelled those words at Savannah. He bagged the last item, an extra pack of bullets. Savannah handed him her credit card. He looked hard at it as if trying to figure out who she was. The card still had her married name.

"What would a, um, fine lady such as you need with all of this ammo?"

"Just a little protection from foul men who like to drive around in their sports cars and bully girls. Like a boy

I used to find so, so hot." Savannah leaned across the counter with a whispery voice. Carl leaned toward her as if drawn by a magnet.

"*Farten*berry, the other girls called him behind his back. They tried to convince me he was a jerk, but I tried to see the good in people. Not anymore, let me tell ya!" She grabbed her bagged purchases and swished out of the store.

"Savannah? Savannah *Banana*?" his voice cracked, and his mouth dropped.

Savannah didn't look back. She couldn't wait to go home and review the video captured on her sunshades— the look on Carl's face when he finally realized who she was as she walked away.

*"Wherefore a lion out of the forest shall slay them,
and a wolf of the evenings shall spoil them, a leopard shall
watch over their cities: every one that goeth out thence shall
be torn in pieces: because their transgressions are many,
and their backslidings are increased."*
—Jeremiah 5:6 (KJV)

CHAPTER THIRTY

Re-watching the video of Carl flirting with Savannah had given her the boost of confidence she was going to need for an extremely risky plan that evening. Savannah knew she would never be able to get any animal tranquilizers unless she robbed a veterinarian clinic. And that was out of the question. The police would keep her behind bars until she died. She planned to fill the tranquilizing darts with enough dosage to sedate the pit bulls if needed.

She remembered from a movie she had seen about the famous New York club kids and how they took ketamine, animal tranquilizers called "special K," to get high and disconnect from their troubles.

Savannah needed to look as convincing and club savvy as she could to pull this off and score the controlled substance. She duct-taped her stomach in and squeezed into the neon-printed bodysuit she had bought for the occasion before pulling on her black wig.

"Ugh, who am I kidding? God, Savannah, you look like a middle-aged hooker," she groaned in front of her bedroom dressing mirror, trying to stretch the fabric from revealing her extra curves. "Those raver kids will all know I've never been inside a nightclub in my whole life."

She painted her face and teetered to her car in her chunky shoes, thankful it was dark so no one could see her. Whenever she drove the highways at night, she couldn't help but see Noel walking the pavement in his little elf costume. She wondered what his last thoughts were—what exactly happened in his final moments. God, if she saw a child on the road, any child, she would break her neck to rescue them, though it would never bring back her son—her whole world.

After twenty minutes, she pulled into the dimly lit parking lot of The Electric Fungeon, the seediest club that Savannah knew of in downtown Birmingham. She parked in the back of the club, where it was the darkest. She could hear the booming music vibrating from the club before she even stepped out of the car. She carefully stepped over beer splatters, discarded cigarettes, used condoms, and colorful metal tubes that looked like either lipstick or eyeliner tubes. Savannah paid the admittance fee at the entry booth and received her plastic wristband like the hospitals use on sick patients.

The farther she went into the club, her whole body throbbed from the pulsing rhythm deep inside the old brick building. It didn't take long to realize that what she had mistaken as eyeliner tubes were disposable vape pens the kids were puffing on in the courtyard.

"Yo, bitches! We got a thirsty boomer comin' up in here," said a teenage boy scratching his crotch. The other kids he called "bitches" turned to face Savannah, who wanted to run back to her car. She had way overdressed. The wild New York club kids she had seen on television weren't anything like they were in Alabama. Many were wearing simple jeans and t-shirts as if standing out in a crowd was a danger now.

"Check out that fit—extra," said a heavyset girl with her butt hanging out of her shorts.

"Yo, boomer mama, you stanning GaGa? Alright then," said another girl with something sparkling on her upper teeth.

Savannah didn't understand half of what they said, but she kept her mind on her goal. They could ridicule her all they wanted; she was going to save some children.

"You want some of this?" asked the guy, still scratching his crotch, while the other kids made lewd comments and gestures.

A guy with long blue hair on the top of his head and shaved sides stepped forward from the crowd. Unlike the others, he was closer to what Savannah had expected with his fishnet shirt and big holes in his earlobes.

"Y'all bitches wished you looked as cool as GaGa here," he said, before leaning close to Savannah and whispering. "Don't let 'em get to ya. You shouldn't've wasted a look like this here, though. You need to be flexing at the gay clubs looking all snatched. That's where I usually go, but I don't wanna run into my ex for a while. I want him to think I've got a fucking life outside our usual circle." He looked around. "But it sure as hell ain't here."

"Snatched?" asked Savannah, unsure of just how she looked.

"You know? Hot—fashionable. I'm Seth Seven. Alright . . . it's Slevin—here anyway." He held out his hand to shake Savannah's.

"You're too kind," she replied. "I'm Valinda, and I'm sorta new around here."

Seth nodded knowingly and sipped on his beer.

"I really need to score some special K. Do you know where I could get any?" whispered Savannah.

"Oh, you mean vitamin K," said Seth. "Yeah, there's a dude here who can hook you up, but you better know, he can be a real prick."

"I don't mind. I need a fix, you know. It's been a rough year. I lost my son. He got bullied for being gay."

Seth's eyes moistened, and his mouth shifted regretfully. "Oh honey, I have been far from the yellow brick road myself. Come on," he said, holding out his arm for her.

Savannah hooked her hand on the crook of his elbow as he strutted into the club. Immediately, Savannah's dress glowed from the blacklights and flashing strobes from the distant dancefloor, which was surprisingly uncrowded. No one seemed to be dancing. Savannah could understand why a lot of the boys weren't dancing; they could hardly walk as it was with their pants sagging to their knees. A skirt would give them more crotch room, but they would rather constantly tug on their pants, she supposed.

Seth said something, but Savannah couldn't hear a thing people were saying. The same handful of digital notes kept repeating maddeningly while a few guys and girls humped each other in the corners. Disposable and forgettable songs compared to the music from every other decade that Savannah could think of. The laughter and smiles she had come to expect were now pissy sulks as though the kids were posing for selfies before a big fight.

Seth craned his neck, searching for the drug dealer. He paused to speak to a man with a hooded t-shirt, who led them down a narrow hall where the restrooms were. He knocked five times, then one more knock. A man twice Seth's build opened the door, releasing a fog of smoke which smelled like a charred skunk, a disgusting blend with the smell of urine and vomit that had seeped below the tiled floor under the toilets.

If anyone had told Savannah a few years earlier that she would be scoring drugs in a teen club meat market, while dressed in a glow-in-the-dark bodystocking, and that she would be stockpiling weapons and plotting a ranch invasion, she would've bet her life that she would never do such things. But the murder of a child can change everything.

"Big D. Whut's up, bro? Yo, there's a bitch here who needs some K," said the man in the hood, pointing at Savannah, who stood beside Seth.

With a wolflike snarl that curled both corners of his

mouth, Big D stood within inches of Savannah and examined her lewdly.

"What makes you think I got any K?" asked Big D.

"I told her you could get her some," said Seth, before he and the hooded man shoved him against the wall.

"Listen up, fuckin' fruitcakes; you in the wrong club. And you don't know me," said Big D, pulling a knife from his pants and holding it under Seth's throat.

"Let him go!" said Savannah. "I'm the one who asked where I could get some special K."

The men shoved Seth to the damp floor and grabbed Savannah. A line of kids was now waiting to get through the blocked hall to use the restroom. Some opened the stall doors to leave but locked themselves back inside when they saw Big D brandishing his knife.

"You expect me to believe that bullshit?" said Big D snatching Savannah's wig off. "You's a muthafuckin' narc."

"No! No, I swear I'm not a police officer. Look, I don't trust them as much as you don't." Savannah held her hands over her face in case he tried to hit her. "I need something to help kill the pain. My, my little boy was murdered, my father died, and my husband left me. Please." Savannah's arms trembled, and the man gave her the wig back. She quickly pulled it over her head.

"If I sell you some K, you gonna take a hit right here in front of me to see if you be lyin'," said Big D, folding his arms threateningly.

Savannah thought her heart would give out. She had no idea what the drug would do to her, especially with having lupus. But she had better not hesitate any longer.

"Yes, the sooner the better," she said. "I need at least a gram, please."

The guy in the hood left and reappeared with a bottle of K, which he handed to Big D.

"You's gonna give me eighty bucks, and if you betray me, I'll kill ya."

Savannah fished a hundred-dollar bill from her purse and told him to keep the change. Big D handed the bottle and a syringe to Savannah. She had no idea how to shoot up. Noticing her awkwardness, the man in the hood grabbed the bottle, inserted the needle, and extracted some of the tranquilizer. While Big D squeezed Savannah's arm until she cried out, the man injected the needle into her bulging vein near her inner elbow.

He tossed the syringe on the floor near Seth and gave her the bottle, which she stuffed in her purse. She knew she had to get the bottle chilled as soon as possible, so she helped Seth off the floor, thanked him, and left the club.

"Oh, goodness. I need to get home before the drug starts taking effect," Savannah mumbled to herself, as she stumbled back to her car. She knew the drug could start working in as little as five minutes.

She opened the trunk of her car, put the bottle of tranquilizer in an ice cooler, and shut the lid tight. When she opened the door to her car, she looked at the windshield and saw that somebody had wedged twelve religious tracts under her left wiper blade. One of the tracts read, "Warning! God and His Army are coming for you!" One tract featured seven trumpets blowing in the clouds and listed all the plagues and disasters caused by each brass horn. The worst pamphlet showed graphic images of people being tortured in Hell, with flames eating their outer flesh. The best tract showed people on a floor of fluffy clouds, bowing down for all of eternity in front of a lily-white God who looked two hundred years old. The church address and affiliation had been inked out as usual.

"Damn you! Who keeps doing this? Where are you? Show yourself, you coward!" Savannah yelled, after stepping back out of her car. The pain in her joints had vanished, but she felt like she was floating in outer space now. The earthshaking bass from the club music had become a pleasant hum. Savannah felt like a waitress at a drive-in as she mazed through the parking lot, hoping to find religious pamphlets on any of the other vehicles. She tried to focus. The cars seemed enormous now, too large to even see the windshields. She grabbed hold of a front bumper to keep from falling, or was it the car's roof?

"She's in a K-hole," said some man standing over her. "I think he gave her too much."

"We can't leave her here in the parking lot. Help me lift her," said another man.

Savannah felt like a dozen angels were lifting her to the black heavens. She hadn't felt this good in years.

"Valinda, are you okay?" asked a man with blue hair, squatting beside her as she leaned against the brick wall of the club.

"Who's Valinda?" mumbled Savannah.

"You are. It's me—Seth. Do you need me to take you

home?"

"Where am I?"

"You're at The Electric Fungeon."

"How long have I been here?" she asked, looking up at the cars in the lot.

"About an hour now," said Seth.

Savannah used all her strength to stand, but her knees buckled. Seth placed his arm around her back and steadied her.

"No, thanks. I want to drive myself home," she said, slowly getting her bearings.

Seth helped Savannah to her car and closed the door for her. "Oh, you dropped a bunch of these little pamphlets. I'm not sure if you wanted 'em or not," said Seth. "They look pretty disturbing, to be honest."

Savannah rolled down her window and took the tracts. "The church that killed my baby boy keeps leaving them—they keep stalking me everywhere. I was trying to catch them when I collapsed."

"Sounds like my family. When they found out I was gay, they said they'd rather see me dead in the street. I haven't seen them since then. Which is fine, I guess. I lived in fear they were going to put poison in my food or something. Are you sure you're going to be okay?" asked Seth, noticing the rip in his shirt the drug dealers had caused. He smoothed back his rumpled hair.

"Don't you worry about me. Are you okay?" Savannah couldn't believe the poor boy's awful family story. No wonder so many gay kids turn to drugs, she imagined.

Seth flicked his hand dismissively. "Yeah. I guess I asked for it, coming here tonight and all."

"That's not true. You should be able to go anywhere you want to without being mistreated or shunned."

Seth turned sideways, and Savannah grabbed him by his wrist.

"Listen to me, baby," she said. "You're too good for this hell hole. Sometimes we have to love ourselves because the world just can't."

Seth blinked rapidly as a smile spread over his face. "Thank you, Ms. Valinda. I hope you find happiness soon." He reached through the open driver's window and hugged her.

Savannah drove home as carefully as possible, watching for police and stalkers. She would rather face pit bulls than ever return to that den of wolves, no matter if they had the word "fun" in their name illuminated with three times the neon lights.

"That whosoever would not seek the Lord God of Israel should be put to death, whether small or great, whether man or woman."
—2 Chronicles 15 (KJV)

CHAPTER THIRTY-ONE

Visions of the boy fleeing the Santa Shack had vexed Savannah's waking thoughts. There was no time to delay. She had to get one last thing; she had to find somebody connected with the media—a major news channel preferably—to cover the story to the very end. She was going to have to step over the local media and authorities to do so. They couldn't be trusted.

Savannah spent hours and hours searching for controversial news stories online. She was looking for somebody brave enough to cover a story that other newsgroups wouldn't touch with a fifty-foot holy scepter. She made notes of any prospects, but they were few.

"Reagan Maddox with EJSBC!" Savannah said triumphantly. "Women are far braver these days about speaking out against controversial injustices."

She had forgotten that Maddox was one of the top news reporters to cover the news story that should have shocked the nation. But everyone Savannah knew had remained oddly unaware, or at least they chose to keep quiet, which was a sign of privilege and approval, Savannah had come to learn over time.

Three presidential candidates in 2016: Tod Crane, Mark Huckenstein, and Bonnie Jinkins had attended a Religious Liberties Conference in Iowa under keynote speaker Ken Swayze, a Dominionist pastor, who included those three candidates in his rally cry to "Kill the Gays." Swayze's supporters had suggested bringing back old-fashioned biblical stoning death penalties for gay people. The rally distributed pamphlets suggesting dominionists might even get the government to consider throwing gay people off buildings as an alternative to restore righteousness to America. It was all there, the entire rally caught on video, and Reagan Maddox with EJSBC had begged other major news networks to at least acknowledge the shocking event.

And that event was just what Marjorie had tried to warn Savannah about. She didn't recognize the underlying mission of the campaign rally back then. They want to establish the church in the theonomy they claim God has been waiting for, thus allowing Him to come back and reign over His re-established theocracy with power-hungry politicians sitting at His right hand. But some truths must remain silent, and some groups must remain protected. See no evil, speak no evil, hear no evil, or at least justify the evil.

Savannah blocked her number and called *EJSBC News* and told them about everything that had happened to her son and everything Marjorie had told her. The assistant put her on hold, and to Savannah's surprise, Reagan Maddox decided to take over the call. Savannah re-explained everything to her.

"I have video evidence they are abusing boys, and I would have more, but the sheriff made me leave. I'm going to break on to the property tomorrow morning to prove it. But before I tell you who I am or where I'm located, I need your word that you'll be willing to cover this story."

"I'm speaking with Savannah Graysen. I know who this is," said Reagan.

Savannah's vision blurred, and she felt like she had been sucked up into a vortex. "H-How did you—"

"While you were telling me everything, I looked up some of the details about your son's murder—how he was left in a manger. I'm sorry about your loss. But look, Savannah, I'm not saying I don't believe you; I just need to see this evidence you claimed to have captured before we commit to covering this story. Can you text me the video clip? I'll remain on hold."

Reagan gave Savannah her private cell number, and Savannah attached the video and hit send.

"I just got it, and I'm opening it now. Hold on," said Reagan.

"It's near the very end—the boy running out of the Santa Shack." Savannah got chills of hope.

"Oh, okay. I see. Hmmm, let me slow this down and have another look. Okay, here's the thing, Savannah. This video doesn't prove child abuse, unfortunately. People will look at it and think the boy is running from an outhouse because he got stung by a bee on the toilet or something. No one is chasing him."

Savannah gritted her teeth. "But what about the blood on him? He looked traumatized."

"People will think the boy sat on a nail or played with a firecracker or something. You know the saying people use to excuse male misbehavior: 'Boys will be boys.'"

Reagan ended the call. Savannah let out a long sigh of disgust and disappointment. She felt too defeated to try another news organization. And some crackpot kid with a camera on a podcast at 3:AM wouldn't be sufficient to override biased news organizations, maybe fifty years after she died, it might, but neither Savannah nor the children could wait for that.

The living room clock chimed noon, and the doorbell rang twelve times. Savannah peeped through the viewing hole in the door as her blood rushed through her chilled veins. Somebody was blocking the hole with a black Bible. Savannah wouldn't dare open it this time.

"Who is it?" she yelled through the locked door.

"Just a lowly servant of the Lord, ma'am."

"What do you want?"

"God wants you to use your free will and let Him into your heart so he can redeem you," said the man, who sounded in his early twenties or younger.

"Redeem me from what?" asked Savannah, keeping her ear pressed to the door and trying to remain calm. "I don't have any children left to torture and kill."

"God wants to redeem you from the Hell he created for people who refuse him. Are you going to refuse Him?

This might be your last chance. Aaaall you need to do is let Jesus get one foot inside your door, ma'am."

One foot was twelve inches, Savannah realized. This was another code word for Twelfthtide.

"This doesn't sound like free will to me. It sounds like a terrorist threat. Are you threatening me?" asked Savannah.

"None of us are promised tomorrow, Mrs. Graysen. Anyway, I know you've been talking to the lesbians. Gay people are an enemy of God, and your son, no matter how sweet he was, was an abomination."

Savannah clutched her jittery stomach. At last, the snake admitted to knowing her name. He had to be one of the people following her or the one who stole her car. But how dare he say such a thing about her dead son?

"Get off—get off my property!" sputtered Savannah. She yelled so hard she thought she had damaged her vocal cords. Her body vibrated as she pounded and kicked the door. "Don't ever come here again. Damn you!"

She slid to the floor and covered her mouth with her hands to muffle her cries. After a few minutes of silence, Savannah felt she had better call Marjorie. The woman needed to know what had happened, whether she refused to get involved or not.

The call went into voicemail. Savannah rattled off the past events as fast as she could in case the phone message time limit ended.

"I swear, Marjorie; I don't know how he knew I talked to you guys. It felt so threatening. I know what the video captured. I'm going to Canaan Land Acres first thing tomorrow. If you don't ever hear from me again, you'll know they got me. Take care and keep safe, my friend."

*"Go ye after him through the city, and smite:
let not your eye spare, neither have ye pity:
Slay utterly old and young, both maids, and
little children, and women: but come not near any man
upon whom is the mark; and begin at my sanctuary."*
—Ezekiel 9 (KJV)

CHAPTER THIRTY-TWO

The alarm clock went off at five in the morning. Savannah got up and put on her bulletproof vest first, then her camouflage coveralls and hat she had bought online. If she got pulled over, it wouldn't be too unusual for anyone to be dressed in hunting gear in the South, except Savannah was hunting for humans—no, she took that back; she was hunting for monsters, evil monsters.

She guzzled an energy drink, ate a protein bar, and began gathering all her equipment. She secured the spare hidden camera on the top button of her coveralls, and on her belt, she clipped on her assassin's knife just in case. She made sure her pistol was fully loaded, and the spare bullets were in a holder on the other side of her belt. In one of the oversized pockets near her knees, she put the cans of bear spray. Lastly, she grabbed her tranquilizer gun and juiced-up darts in their cooler.

Before walking out the door, she sent a text to her mother on her fully charged cellphone. She was certain it would be the last time she would get to tell her mom that she loved her. Savannah couldn't call her; Molly would know something was up by the fear in her voice. Mothers always knew these things. Savannah didn't need any opposition to hamper her mission. She had made up her mind.

The sky was barely bright enough to see when Savannah parked on the road in front of Canaan Land Acres. The dew-covered vegetation smelled like fresh-cut hay. Only a rooster somewhere in the distance disturbed the silence, except for the crunching gravel under her boots, which seemed to echo for a mile. Savannah loaded the darts in the tranquilizing gun and grabbed some slabs of raw meat, which she infused with her own concoction of tranquilizer serum. If she could take the dogs down long enough, she might have a chance to see if Joseph and Jud really were child abductors and killers. She lifted the binoculars around her neck and began searching for the pit bulls. They must still be asleep, she figured, as she climbed over the gate to the ranch. She started walking up the gravel road between the iron crosses flanking both sides. Savannah had an unnerving thought. What if the crosses were grave markers where Joseph had buried his victims?

The butterbean patch to her left rattled, and a growl startled her. The pit bull lunged at Savannah so fast it was too late to get a good aim with the tranquilizer gun. The dog bit down on her leg, puncturing one of the cans of bear spray, which started hissing in the pocket of her coveralls. Savannah dropped all the slabs of meat. She couldn't block the fumes of bear spray, now seeping through the camouflage fabric of her coveralls, and shoot the dog at the same time. The dog jumped back and vomited from the taste of the bear spray, giving Savannah just enough time to run back the way she came. How she managed to jump the gate without being able to see or breathe was a miracle. Her eyes were pouring water and burning from the filtered fumes. She couldn't imagine enduring a direct misting of the bear spray. She reached inside her pocket, grabbed the leaking can, and flung it as far inside the garden as she could.

She crawled to the trunk of her car, opened the door, reached inside the ice chest, and began sloshing ice and water on her face and hands and even up her nostrils.

She was awake now if she hadn't ever been before, but the only problem was, so were Joseph and Jud probably. Farmers usually wake up before sunrise, even if the barking dogs didn't alert them.

She sat on the gravel and gasped for air, worrying if she was in the middle of the road or the side. Luckily, she didn't hear any cars coming, but a pack of dogs was now furiously barking as if they were fighting. A few minutes later, everything grew quiet.

"Haaa. Come on, Savannah. You can do this," she gasped as hard as she could to clear her lungs. Though she felt like she had just sustained third-degree burns, she closed the trunk, grabbed her tranquilizer gun, and crouched in front of the gate before going any farther. She looked through her binoculars and noticed several patches of colorful fur on the gravel drive. The patches were the pit bulls, and they were as stiff as boulders. Savannah realized they must have fought over the raw meat and, in the process, had swallowed enough tranquilizer. Now was her best shot at getting inside the ranch.

She jumped the gate and walked as fast as her legs could go. Moving in intervals, dodging from one old pecan tree trunk to another, she paused the longest behind a tractor. Breaking into the ranch house wasn't a good idea. She wanted to check out something smaller first, the Santa Shack.

She crept up to the hideous building, which was just a little bigger than most outhouses. The Santa Clauses painted on the building had eyes and grins like serial killer John Wayne Gacy in his infamous clown makeup. The reindeer had glowing red eyes and extra-sharp horns. The little elves sprinkled between them looked like demonic imps. Savannah made sure no one was looking and pulled the door handle, which was actually a red nose on one of the painted reindeer. She entered the shack and closed the door. The walls were painted with similar Christmas jollies, just as disturbing as the ones outside. A sturdy wooden bench jutted from the floor in the back of the shack, and a sliding bolt secured the inside of the door. Now, why would children need to lock themselves inside a Santa Shack?

"No, Reagan Maddox with EJSBC, this sure as hell is not an outhouse," muttered Savannah bitterly.

She hoped her button camera was capturing all of this as it was still too dark outside to wear her camera sunglasses. A bare red lightbulb suspended from the ceiling, but that wasn't all—ropes hung from the top as well. And what were all the levers for on the far side of the bench? Savannah tested them: One lever lowered and raised the ropes. One caused the wall panels to slide back, revealing what Savannah could only describe as horned Christmas devils. One lever caused red flames to shoot from Santa's laughing mouth. Savannah pushed a red nose protruding on another reindeer.

"HO-HO-HO-HA-HE-HAA!" The button had activated a laughing growl so sick Savannah thought she would vomit. What type of hell did children endure in this shack? She spotted a jar of petroleum jelly in the far corner of the structure. But there was no time to linger; she needed to find the children before anyone caught her.

Savannah headed toward the towering barn next. The only way to get inside it that she could see was the front door, which was barricaded with a giant iron cross. She dodged behind the barn when Jud Mason Weeks walked out of the house with a massive bag of dog food.

A terrible fluttering traveled through Savannah. It surely wouldn't take long for Jud to realize the dogs weren't coming for their morning breakfast, and he would find them sedated. Entering through the barn door was too risky now. Jud began whistling and calling for the dogs. Savannah crept farther behind the barn and saw a window. It was too high up, so she started stacking bales of hay against the wall until she could climb up and reach the window. Jud was still whistling, thankfully. Savannah pushed and pulled on the window, but it wouldn't open. She pressed her face against the dirty glass and nearly fell backward off the top bale. In the far corner of the barn were about a dozen boys chained to the wall in tattered robes with several gruesome crucifixes towering over them.

Somebody sounded a bell. It must be Jud alerting Joseph. Savannah pressed the camera up against the glass, hoping to get a better recording of the boys. She pulled out her phone and took photos as well. Then she speed-dialed Marjorie. She didn't answer, so Savannah waited for the beep.

"Marjorie! Marjorie, I'm at the ranch. We were right. Joseph and Jud Weeks have at least a dozen boys chained up in the big barn behind their house. They looked awful." Savannah's voice cracked from tears and fear. "Somebody just sounded an alarm. I don't know what else to do. I don't know how I'm going to be able to get back to my car now."

Savannah ended the call and sent the video clips and photos to Reagan Maddox with EJSBC. She added the message. "I was right. Joseph Weeks has kidnapped boys, and he's holding them on his ranch. I can't leave. Please just know this is the truth."

Her fingers were shaking so bad she hoped Reagan could read her typing. Savannah got a brilliant idea if it would work.

She elbowed one of the panes in the window, breaking it. The startled boys looked up at her and began praying. She grabbed her camera sunshades from her chest pocket, reached her arm inside the broken glass, and threw the shades as hard as she could toward the boys. The shades didn't quite reach them and landed between the crosses instead. Savannah pointed at the glasses. "Get them and put them on." She pointed to her eyes. One of the boys stretched his arm forward, but the chain on his ankle was too short for him to reach.

"No, Simon Peter, the Bible says we aren't supposed to have possessions—says it in Luke 12," said a taller boy. He grabbed Simon and flung him back against the wall.

The door to the barn creaked open. Joseph Weeks entered and walked around with a gun, looking for any intruders. After he had searched every object large enough for a human to hide behind, he stood in front of the boys.

"Where are they? I know you've seen them," he yelled, squinting his eyes.

The boys huddled together and trembled. Then Joseph looked down between the crosses and saw the sunshades. He grabbed them up. "Where did these come from?" he screamed.

Savannah was silently pleading that they wouldn't tell on her, but three of the boys pointed up at her.

"The Devil's harlot . . . up there in the window, Father," said one of the boys.

Every nerve in Savannah's body stung as she began climbing down the hay bales as fast as she could. She ran back toward the front gate when she paused. Blue lights were flashing in the distance toward the road. Sheriff Johnny-Dale Larson must have arrived on the scene, for he was pointing his gun at Jud Weeks and frisking him as he leaned against the tractor. Marjorie had been wrong about the sheriff.

"You evil swine. You raped and killed my son! That's him, Sheriff Larson," growled Savannah, stomping up to Jud with her gun aimed at him. "That's Jud Mason Weeks, and his father is in the barn with the other boys they kidnapped."

Jud turned around and hugged the sheriff. "Thanks for showing me how to frisk heathens, Mr. Larson," said Jud with a sick grin.

"Drop the gun NOW, Savannah," ordered Sheriff Larson. "Go get 'er boy." He shoved Jud toward her.

Savannah refused to drop the gun; she aimed it at Jud, determined to kill him, determined to keep him from hurting other children. Her hand began to shake.

"Jud, wait. Listen to me: These people are lying to you. You are not Joseph's son. Your real father is Pastor J.R. Morris of Athens, Georgia. Joseph abducted you during a Christmas parade when you were little."

"Don't listen to her, Jud. Satan is the father of lies," said Sheriff Larson.

"They're using you. I'm afraid you, you've forgotten what real love is. Don't you remember having a mother once? Having her hold you—kiss you goodnight?" Savannah struggled between seeing Jud as the monster he now was and the innocent child who had been brainwashed into hate and violence. She realized she had lowered her gun.

Jud took two more steps forward, and a loud *POP*

came from the gate. Bloody brains and skull bones splattered from Jud's head. His eyes enlarged before he fell face forward inches from Savannah's feet. She looked to her left and couldn't believe her husband had found her at the ranch, much less that he had just pulled the trigger of his shotgun.

Sheriff Larson swung to the right and aimed his gun at Scotty. "What have you done, Scotty? You gave us your word that you had turned your back on the wicked world and had become a Twelfthtide Disciple. But you're just another Judas."

"Oh, Scotty. You mean you were a part of this—this evil movement?"

Scotty's face began to twitch and turn red. He stifled a cry, which escaped like a sneeze. "I . . . I'm sorry, Savannah. I'm so sorry."

A series of loud gunshots rattled off. Scotty's body jarred backward as he received one bullet after the other before collapsing near one of the sleeping pit bulls.

Savannah dropped to her aching knees. Preparing to die herself, she looked up into the sky and thought her tears had distorted her vision at first. A team of helicopters came over the treetops and hovered over the ranch.

"This is the FBI. Drop your gun and put your hands behind your head," a woman yelled through a speakerphone at Sheriff Larson from one of six black helicopters. A white and blue helicopter with the words *EJSBC News* landed in the sheep pen and continued filming.

Thank goodness their headquarters was close by in

Atlanta, Savannah realized. They must've believed her story the first time and were already on alert. She was still in disbelief that her husband was dead and that he had been a member of Joseph's group, part of a killer church.

"I'd so hoped you'd join us. And after God took your firstborn and all, you still wouldn't repent," growled Sheriff Larson. He grabbed Savannah by her hair and snatched her to her feet.

"God didn't kill him; you all did," said Savannah, feeling as though he was about to break her neck and snatch her baldheaded as he dragged her toward the ranch house, using her as a human shield. The helicopters swarmed like hornets, and the FBI took a couple of shots that luckily missed Savannah.

"Same thing, you harlot. God expects his children to do the killings, as acts of obedience—to purge the evil."

"Why, you bastard?" Savannah wheezed in pain. "Is He too lazy to do all the killings since we have cameras these days?"

Sheriff Larson squeezed his left arm harder around her throat. "Because of you sinful children of Adam, God lost control of the Earth to Satan. Now He has given us latter-day prophets and apostles like Father Joseph to teach God's Great Commission to take dominion of this planet back from Satan. You are of your father the devil, but there is no more sacrifice for sin left for you now. God's Army will have their way with you."

Savannah's body was finally at an angle where she was able to slip the knife out of her pocket. With as much force as she could conjure, she shoved the tip of the knife into the sheriff's leg.

With a yell, he released her and grabbed the wound. Savannah didn't take time to think; she ran back toward the gate and instantly heard a hailstorm of bullets rattling around her.

A bullet struck her in the back and knocked her to the ground. It hurt to breathe. She wasn't sure if the bullet had penetrated her bulletproof vest, but it sure felt like it.

An FBI agent came from the side of the ranch house and grabbed Sheriff Larson, shoved him to the ground, and handcuffed him. Savannah looked over at her husband, sprawled on the dirt as she was. His dead eyes seemed to be looking right at her, begging forgiveness.

"FBI, ma'am. Are you Savannah Graysen?" asked a female agent leaning over her in her camouflage uniform and vest.

"Yes," she said, as the agent checked her for injuries and helped her to her feet. "Don't worry about me; you have to help the boys. Th-there are about twelve of them chained up in the barn. Joseph Weeks was inside it last I saw him. He, he has a gun."

"Think hard, Mrs. Graysen. Are there any other perpetrators that you know of?"

"Joseph Weeks has followers everywhere—especially in the local law enforcement who might be a threat," replied Savannah, stretching her cramping leg and back.

"You already reported that to *EJSBC News*. I mean any perpetrators here on the ranch."

"I don't know. Not that I'm aware of," answered Savannah. "I didn't get a chance to search inside the house, though."

The woman relayed Savannah's information to the FBI on her walkie talkie. One agent was lowered on the roof of the barn while another helicopter landed behind it.

A paramedic removed Savannah's vest and checked her for wounds. "No visible flesh wounds," she said, checking her pulse and making her take a few deep breaths. "There are signs of skin irritation. Were you exposed to any type of nerve agent that you know of, Mrs. Graysen?"

"I don't think so. It's probably my lupus. I'm not supposed to be in the sun."

One of the three reporters with *EJSBC News*, who had been filming the chaos, turned off his camera when he approached Savannah. "I'm Jared Ferguson, investigative journalist with *EJSBC News*. I must say, your story seems to be adding up," he said. "This is all going live, so there'd better be evidence of the kidnapped children, or there's going to be a shitstorm of legality issues."

"I'm telling you: the children are in the barn. I have the recording on my computer. Somebody needs to get those boys out," said Savannah. She took a few steps toward the barn, but the paramedic pulled her into a shaded area near the gate.

"Calm down, Mrs. Graysen. It's our job to protect you. We will get to the bottom of it," said the FBI agent.

"The FBI won't let *EJSBC News* near the barn yet, but it is important that you let us see the recordings first. You can trust me; I'm not an FBI agent posing as a journalist," the reporter said to Savannah.

The female agent's face formed a slight scowl at the journalist's comment. In the distance, another agent removed the cross blocking the barn door, and he slipped inside the structure with his gun drawn.

"I'm only comfortable handing the recordings over to Reagan Maddox. What made you decide to respond? Was it the photos I sent her earlier?" Savannah asked the journalist, still unsure if she could trust him any more than the FBI.

The journalist checked over his notes. "I understand. You aren't the only person fearing for your life because of the Twelfthtide organization, Mrs. Graysen. Around three this morning, an informant claiming to be a former employee with the sheriff's department sent *EJSBC News* a copy of police records featuring data taken from your husband's computer. Scotty Graysen joined Joseph Weeks's church through their online website twelve years ago—a website moderated by Sheriff Johnny-Dale Larson designed to recruit members who type in certain keywords used by extremists. There were lots of emails exchanged between Scotty and Larson. Scotty particularly liked their anti-gay and anti-minority teachings. Sheriff Larson hooked up Scotty with one of the Twelfthtide members named Pam Ragland."

"She's the mother of their child together—the son Scotty really wanted," said Savannah, trembling with regret.

"At some point, Scotty apparently had a change of heart about getting rid of all his worldly possessions and wanted to make a go with his own car dealership. They weren't happy when Scotty started turning his back on the church. Over time, the emails became more demanding for Scotty to do something to prove his faith in God and Prophet Joseph. The Twelfthtide Apostolics were trying to get Scotty to see the wickedness of celebrating pagan holidays like Christmas, Easter, and Halloween and allowing women to have any say about anything. Then Joseph and Johnny-Dale started trying to blackmail him. After Noel was murdered, the local law enforcement agreed to release Scotty as a suspect and cover up his ties to the Twelfthtide Disciples if he agreed not to leave or disparage the church."

Savannah felt as though she had been the dumbest housewife on the planet. "I can't believe what I'm hearing. He, he never told me he had joined any church. Of course, I didn't know he had another woman and a child either."

"I've researched these matters for years. Scotty's case sounds like an uncle of mine who joined an extremist type church," said the journalist. "Finding God isn't always the motivation; it's eradicating all the things in life you hate that make sinners and saints strange bedfellows."

The female FBI agent answered her walkie talkie and a frown deepened on her face. She turned to Savannah and the cameraman. "FBI couldn't find Joseph Weeks. Are you sure you saw him in the barn, Mrs. Graysen?"

"Yes. He must be hiding, or he escaped," answered Savannah, fearing they would think she had made up everything. She watched with relief when three FBI agents rushed the boys out of the barn and into a circle of other officers.

"There! There see; I told you," cried Savannah, pointing at the boys as a bilious knot of pain and worry decreased in her stomach.

The journalist lifted his camera and filmed the rescue.

If only one of the freed boys had been Noel. At least he could have survived, Savannah wished. As though he recognized her, one of the older boys sat on a manger filled with hay and stared at her through the iron crosses lining the driveway. Savannah got chills. Did he want her to remember the crime scene photos of Noel?

CHAPTER THIRTY-THREE

Savannah turned off her favorite local news channel with a sick heaviness returning. Marjorie was right about the scope of danger they faced. Only Reagan Maddox dared tell the truth on *EJSBC News*. The local channels refused to report the Twelfthtide Apostolics as the growing religious movement it was. Instead, they claimed the usual: White men with mental illness on one channel; lone gunmen with chips on their shoulders, who just needed God, on another channel; and unredeemable child predators on yet another. And though *EJSBC News* had been careful to protect Savannah's identity, the local stations outed her and Scotty as the informants seeking vengeance for Noel's death. But they somehow avoided mentioning Casey De Grasse, whose son, Joseph and Jud had killed and left in a manger as well. And even that act, the local news claimed, was not a religious omen but a hate crime against religion, a blasphemous act. Savannah was hopeful the investigations into the local police and sheriff's department would yield proof of their involvement with Joseph's church if any.

She was still in so much pain from the following day; she couldn't bring herself to sweep up the dead needles from the Christmas tree. She went to the kitchen to take a pain pill when her cellphone rang.

"Oh, it's probably Mom worried about me again," she said, before answering the call.

"Thank goodness you answered. This is Marjorie. I'm in your area and need to talk to you. I think you are in danger."

"Why? What's going on?"

"Joseph Weeks is still missing, for one thing. I sneaked inside Canaan Land Acres to do my own research. I found a hidden room inside the ranch house—a sanctuary, I believe. There was an altar in the room with the scripture from Deuteronomy written in blood."

"What Scripture?"

"A scripture about God being jealous and punishing several generations of grandkids for something their parents did."

"It doesn't matter, Marjorie. I'll never have any more children."

"That's not exactly my point, Savannah. I found a photo of Scotty, Noel, and you on the altar. They have already killed Scotty and your son. Joseph will not rest until he comes for you now. I'll be there in a minute."

"Okay," said Savannah, hanging up. She changed out of her robe and slippers and into something more presentable when the doorbell rang.

Savannah hobbled as fast as she could to the door and opened it just a little to make sure it was Marjorie. The door smacked her in the forehead and knocked her to the floor.

Standing over her was a man in his sixties with a long beard, long sleeves, and a large rock in his hand. Savannah was afraid to make any sudden attempt to get off the floor. He could crush her skull just by releasing the rock.

"I suppose you know who I am?" said Joseph Weeks. "You thought you could tear down God's Kingdom, but the gates of Hell shall not prevail against us. We are hidden for now, but soon we will claim dominion. The Bible commands us to stone the disobedient to death." He chunked the rock at Savannah, but she rolled over, receiving only a scratch on the back of her head.

"Devilish little vixen, aren't ya? Maybe I should take you as a concubine," growled Joseph.

"Doesn't that go against your Bible?" hissed Savannah. "I'm not a child virgin!"

"Well, God never gave women a choice; you evil libbers took it, though. Besides, the Bible commands women to be put to death if they don't marry their rapists." Joseph threw himself on top of her and groped her breasts.

Savannah sobbed until he stopped.

"I ain't your type, huh? But I don't want no witch

living with me. You're going to repent once and for all, you are." He jerked her hands behind her back and tied them together with grass rope, which burned her wrists. He then tied her feet and hoisted her into a kneeling position in front of the half-dead Christmas tree.

"I wanna see you pray real good. Ask God to forgive you for this Satan Claws tree you still have up here and for trying to destroy God's true church. And pray He'll go easy on your soul in Hell, which is where I'm about to send you."

"You've already sent me to Hell. Death would be a release from monsters like you," spat Savannah.

Joseph picked up the heavy rock and lifted it above his head, ready to stone Savannah to death.

"Repent, woman! Any person whose arrogant enough to snub the decisions of God's preachers must be killed. Says so in Deuteronomy 17:12."

"I'll never repent," hissed Savannah, coming to a sudden realization. "My son was brave for resisting you and your Twelfthtide Disciples. He's the real hero. And I have no regrets, raising him to love Santa Claus and all. The myths we enjoyed represent far more love and goodness than your myths will ever be capable of."

"Savannah?" a woman's voice called out sheepishly. "Knock, knock; it's me. Are you all right in here?" Marjorie called out, stepping into the living area. Her eyes fixed on Joseph with a look of horror. She reached for her pistol, but he threw the rock, and it smacked her on top of her head. She fell back toward the front door, which remained ajar.

Joseph picked up the bloody rock and once again lifted it over Savannah's head.

"One last time," he growled, while Savannah trembled. "Pray God'll go easy on you for birthing Noel, that abomination you call a hero."

"What did you call my friend?" spat a familiar young voice.

Savannah looked over her shoulder, and an older child with a miniskirt, orange-and-black-striped stockings, and a faded denim jacket had taken Marjorie's pistol from her holster and was aiming it at Joseph. The child was Stacy Beachum, and he stepped carefully over Marjorie's body in his knee-high black boots.

"Get your hillbilly ass away from Mrs. Graysen and carefully climb back under that two-thousand-year-old rock you're holding," said Stacy, with a black-painted snarl.

The sagging muscles around Joseph's eyes clenched with disgust as he eyed Stacy from his teased-out hair to his pointed-toed boots.

"Well now, would you look at that," he gargled. "God help us. This here house is full of abominations!" He lifted the rock high to hurl it at Stacy, but a bullet from the pistol pierced his shoulder, and the rock slipped through his fingers and on his head, then his foot. Dazed, Joseph lifted his arms out as if reaching for support. He stumbled a few steps before falling face down on the floor, smacking his head again on the corner of the coffee table.

"I need something to tie his hands just in case," said Stacy, pacing in circles. His grip on the pistol became shakier as he looked around the living room.

"The tiebacks on the curtains—behind you," said Savannah. "Hurry." She wasn't worried about Joseph reviving and killing her. She was afraid he might kill Stacy and more children. "You're doing great, baby. Stay focused and try not to stress."

Stacy kept the pistol aimed at Joseph while he unhooked the gold curtain cording, embellished with beaded tassels, and tied the man's hands behind his back. "I'd better tie his feet just in case he isn't dead. There," said Stacy, standing up with his hands on his hips. "All bullies could use a little fringe and some jazzy sparkles. It does wonders to cure toxic masculinity; don't you think, Mrs. Graysen." Stacy smirked down at Joseph before rushing over and untying the grass rope on Savannah's hands and feet.

"Thank you, dear," said Savannah. She hobbled over and checked Marjorie's pulse. "Thank heavens! Her heart's still beating, but it's slow. My phone is over there on the kitchen counter, Stacy. Call for an ambulance and just hope they don't refuse us."

"Sure thing," said Stacy. After placing the call, he returned to Savannah's side, holding her phone and looking down at Marjorie with a wilted expression. "Who is she? Is she going to be okay?"

Savannah explained what little she could. "You were really amazing a few minutes ago, Stacy. How did you know I was in trouble?"

"I've been watching your house behind the fence ever since Noel got killed. And I saw the news last night and today. I knew something was up. I was in my treehouse, and I saw Moses over there park his truck down the street and walk to your house, carrying that rock. They showed a photo of him on *EJSBC News*. You were one kick-ass momma how you thought to film everything at the ranch."

Savannah lost her breath and grabbed her chest. "Oh, no!"

Stacy looked around. "What's wrong?"

"We, we just caught Joseph Weeks and I, I forgot to put on my body camera. I'll need proof of everything that happened—proof that Joseph said they were a secret organization that would soon claim dominion."

Stacy pointed up to the video camera mounted at the back of the living room, which was aimed at them. "What about your security camera? Was it on?"

Savannah melted with relief. "*Sheesh*, I'm such an idiot. I was so caught off guard with all of this that I forgot about the cameras."

"Yeah, I thought so." Stacy nodded assuredly, and his earrings jangled. "I saw the company install a security system on your house after Noel died. We have to have a security system, too."

Several sirens grew louder down the street, and Stacy started breathing hard and scratching his arms. "It's the ambulance and FBI. I better leave, or they might put me in jail."

Savannah grabbed his hand, stopping him. "You saved both of our lives. You've every right to be here."

Stacy kept looking back toward the door. "They

won't believe I'm not guilty even if they see the camera recording. The police will know I was involved with stopping Joseph Weeks. They made me keep quiet about this case, remember?"

Savannah felt as though she had been punched in the heart by a flaming fist. Here she finally had a recorded confession from Joseph that would expose the dominionist organization's agenda. But as soon as the police show up to review the recording, they will see that Stacy shot Joseph. Savannah had grown too attached to the child and couldn't risk any more harm coming to him.

"You're right, Stacy. You had better leave through the back door before the cops get here, and don't tell anyone you were ever in this house today." Savannah took the pistol that Stacy had fired and wiped his fingerprints off the weapon before putting her fingerprints on the gun.

Stacy looked up at Savannah with anguished regret before running to the back door. Savannah rushed to the control box for the security camera. She paused with sick dread at what she was about to do. It was insane, in fact. But her heart led her to delete the recording just as the authorities pulled into her driveway.

CHAPTER THIRTY-FOUR

Savannah was devastated. Marjorie slipped into a coma from her head injury, and she might've survived if somebody hadn't unplugged her ventilation machine. The hospital claimed it was an accident when the cleaning crew was mopping the floors. Savannah was certain somebody with the sheriff's department murdered Marjorie, trying to silence her or get revenge. Oddly, no one unplugged Joseph Weeks's breathing machine, and by July of that year, he was released and was awaiting trial.

As usual, the local news stations downplayed the scope of the dominionist organization and still probably would have even if Savannah had kept the recording of Joseph confessing that they were secretly everywhere. Reagan Maddox with *EJSBC News* did mention that Joseph Weeks had confessed about the dominionist movement before he tried to kill Savannah. Politicians and several prominent figures called EJSBC fake news and started fishing for any dirt they could get, hoping to tarnish Reagan's reputation.

The Beachums decided it was in Stacy's best interest

to sell their house and move to Canada.

Savannah finally found somebody willing to hire her—a job as a bookkeeper for the local museum of art. In the first few weeks, the museum received calls from strangers threatening to boycott the museum if they didn't fire "that godless, church-hating Savannah Graysen woman."

Luckily, the owners, originally from Europe, laughed it off and assured Savannah that the callers had probably never set foot inside an art museum. The owners were apparently used to these things.

With religious tracts still appearing on her car windshield and front door to her house, Savannah could never see a life where she could move on, where she didn't have to worry when some new soldier for God would judge her too evil to occupy the planet.

And with Noel, the Beachums, Marjorie, and even Scotty ripped from her life, Savannah couldn't stand the guilt and loneliness. She was so depressed she didn't even know what day it was or what bills were due. She put on one of Noel's favorite records, "Away in a Manger," took a handful of pills, and downed them with a whole bottle of alcohol. The last thing she remembered was collapsing against the dead Christmas tree—the sound of crunching glass ornaments.

"Oh, sweet death, come and take me." If she woke up in the real Hell, as many loving souls claimed she would, at least she had spared twelve boys from this one.

THE END

ABOUT THE AUTHOR

Multi-Award-Winning Author Milan Sergent studied creative writing in college and began writing the novel series "Candlewicke 13" in 2007, a year after featuring some of the series' characters in his solo art exhibition, titled "Outsiders and Apparitions," near Rockefeller Center in New York City.

An artist and poet since adolescence, a few of Sergent's early poetic works were published in *Scarlet Literary Magazine* and more recently in his two illustrated poetry books.

To learn more about the author or his works, visit http://www.milansergent.com. While there, join the mailing list for important news updates and notifications about future novel releases.

ALSO AVAILABLE BY MILAN SERGENT

Dang Near Royal

When the Gurneys receive a visit from a reality show producer, bringing news of a life-changing inheritance, they must choose to go down with their crumbling shack in rural Mississippi or try to pass themselves off as British aristocracy.

Will the dangerous conspiracy theories the elusive Gurneys cling to prove true when many try to convince them that they are victims of human trafficking being exploited in a snuff film?

Praise for *Dang Near Royal*

"Dang Near Royal by Milan Sergent had me in stitches. . . . This is the deep south meeting stuck-up toffee-nosed Britain and it is comedy at its finest. We get to know the amazing, colorful characters very well and some of them you will really get to know – you'll soon know whose side you are on! . . . This is all go right from the first page, a truly down-to-earth comedy with a touch of the bittersweet to it. Milan has written a story that you can only truly appreciate if you understand British humor. I do and I think this would go down a treat as a made-for-TV series in the UK."   —Anne-Marie Reynolds for *Readers' Favorite*

"Dang Near Royal by Milan Sergent is one of the best comedy novels I have read for a long time. I found the clever play on words and the results of miscommunication throughout the plot absolutely hysterical. The characters each had unique personality traits which made for some incredibly humorous interactions. . . . The comedy was consistently witty and sharp. This novel, however, is far more than a continuous stream of slapstick and hilarious situations; there are also wonderful relationship developments, and the bonds between the members of the Gurney family were completely endearing. The ending was a really good example of the importance of trusting your basic instinct when it comes to evaluating the goodness in people. I highly recommend this novel to anyone who loves well-thought-out and intelligent humour."

—Lesley Jones for Readers' Favorite

"Dang Near Royal is a satirical dramedy written by Milan Sergent.... Funny, clever, and at times surprisingly poignant, Dang Near Royal is delightfully outrageous. Milan Sergent's novel is tightly-paced and provides ample entertainment from start to finish. I gobbled it up in one sitting and just couldn't put it down. The characters are quirky and colorful, and despite their inherent flaws, you can't help but root for them. . . . In his quest for humor, author Milan Sergent pulls no punches and makes fun of both southern stereotypes and English aristocracy in equal measure. Dang Near Royal is an absolute riot that I would readily recommend to anybody itching for a hysterically funny read."

—Pikasho Deka for Readers' Favorite

". . . This is a dark comedy that boldly addresses the unthinkable. In an age where many of us are weaned on mindless reality TV programs, Dang Near Royal reminds us that our gullibility can lead to our downfall. I am impressed by Sergent's daring and frank illustration of the exploitative world of reality television. He gives you a thorough look at how the minds of his characters work in a plot that operates like a sitcom. Perhaps the hidden message in Dang Near Royal is that reality television is nowhere close to simulating reality and that it is even getting worse at representing the real world. This novel becomes a must-read, because its balanced drama and humor are relevant, and you want to find out if the Gurneys will emerge from that veil of superficiality."

—Vincent Dublado for Readers' Favorite

"As a first-time reader of Milan Sergent, I certainly was not disappointed. Dang Near Royal is a laugh-out-loud book with elements of realism about the everyday concept we have of the lower side of aristocracy, always making more of themselves than is absolutely necessary. Milan Sergent brings the characters to life with all their foibles, making you have a real feeling of love or loathing for each one. He goes to great lengths to bring what would otherwise be an outrageous story into the realm of humor and succeeds wholeheartedly in making you laugh and cry with frustration at people's antics.... A wonderfully written, funny, and sad book that will make your heart rejoice in the end!"

—Bernadette Diane Anderson for Readers' Favorite

Outsiders and Apparitions

The Pitrick family picnic went off without a hitch until Patty drove the unwelcome wagon into a roadside ditch. Her daughter cried out with maddening dread while apparitions appeared high overhead. She didn't take it as a sign that Patty was dead, but that the crash had mashed her sauerkraut sandwich.

Outsiders and Apparitions: Possessed Poems and Art for Family Picnics by Milan Sergent is an eclectic book of poetry and art by an easily bored author and artist who broke free from gross boundary violations, conformity demands, and abandonment as a youth. The past now only apparitions: he is currently possessed with a mission to encourage expression without dull traditions, rules, or shackling expectations. The soul can be possessed, but the product it produces must be free to protest.

Praise for *Outsiders and Apparitions*
Possessed Poems and Art for Family Picnics

"This superb collection of poetry and art, Outsiders and Apparitions by Milan Sergent, cleverly confronts societal opinions on outward success, happiness, and inner fulfillment. . . . Each poem is illustrated with the most extraordinary and exceptional artwork. I was absolutely captivated by this collection. Milan is such an inspirational artist and writer. His talent for provoking thought and change in human behavior is superb. . . ."
—Lesley Jones for *Readers' Favorite*

"This is the best book of poetry that I have read this year. I absolutely enjoyed the ingenious poetry that Sergent brought to life in this collection. . . . What I loved even more was the collection of paintings that accompanied each poem. . . . Overall, I think Milan Sergent has created a masterpiece. . . . It's definitely a collection I would recommend. I can't wait to read more of his work."
—Tiffany Ferrell for *Readers' Favorite*

"[A] fabulous combination of art and poems that are unique, fresh, and unconventional and take readers to another realm altogether. . . . The collection is eclectic, unapologetic, and fantastical, and is a good way to make readers break free from their traditional ways of expressing themselves and to try out something different."
—Mamta Madhavan for *Readers' Favorite*

"Sergent brings a unique brand of surrealism to an emotionally resonant space in this collection, which explores personal and wider themes that play with structure and form in poetry, but also express a breakout from the conventions of language, art, and society. . . . Having been an ardent fan of Milan Sergent's fiction work for quite some time now, it was a delight to explore another facet of the author's mind and see his artistic process come to light in new forms. . . . Outsiders and Apparitions is a book that no poetry fan should be without."
—K.C. Finn for *Readers' Favorite*

"Milan Sergent's Outsiders and Apparitions is a collection of poetry and artwork that has a way of digging into almost all of your senses. His poetry has a lyrical, children's nursery rhyme sort of bent, but with an adult flavor and tone. An antiquated essence also paints every page, so that there is a feeling of transportation that takes us centuries back into the past."
—Erin Nicole Cochran for *Readers' Favorite*

Martyrs and Manifestations

This is an eclectic book of poetry and art by an easily bored author and artist who broke free from gross boundary violations, conformity demands, and abandonment in his youth.

With oppressive forces still clawing from the grave, and people who try to shame or silence victims and embarrassing history, Sergent is currently on a mission to encourage expression without dull traditions, rules, or shackling expectations. Authoritarians can leave us feeling hexed, but you can break the spell.

Praise for Martyrs and Manifestations
Hexed Poems and Art for Holiday Gatherings

"As a fan of Milan Sergent in general, I anticipated getting into another excellent collection of verses and art, and I was once again thoroughly impressed. . . . There is a really quirky mix of traditionalism and celebration of the poetic form which Sergent cleverly subverts and twists into new rule-breaking permutations to delight and surprise his readers. . . . The underlying themes, empathy, and emotional quality of the work are second to none, clearly coming from a real place within the author which we marginalized folk can all relate to. Overall, I would highly recommend Martyrs and Manifestations . . . to poetry fans, surrealists, and the oppressed seeking freedom the world over."
—K.C. Finn for *Readers' Favorite*

"Martyrs and Manifestations is indeed a masterpiece and I would recommend it to all poetry lovers to read and appreciate the poet's aesthetic abilities, imagination, and creative mind. It is one of the best poetry collections I have come across in recent times. . . ."
—Mamta Madhavan for *Readers' Favorite*

"A few months ago I read Outsiders and Apparitions and I automatically loved it. It was my favorite book of poetry that I came across this year. It's now a tie between that book of poems and this one. . . ."
—Tiffany Ferrell for *Readers' Favorite*

"Milan Sergent has become a favorite author of mine and, having read the Candlewicke 13 series, I was game for a book of poetry that I was certain wouldn't disappoint. Martyrs and Manifestations offers more than just an anthology of poems; the full-color illustrations are spectacular in their composition and vivid hues. . . . Overall, this is an excellent collection that no doubt others will also greatly enjoy."
—Asher Syed for *Readers' Favorite*

"[These poems are] for the brave and daring, and for those too timid to try or speak out. Even if you can't speak or live as brashly as the poems suggest, you can live them vicariously. That's the beauty of poetry, and the beauty of Sergent's work. . . . If you're looking for poetry for the holidays that isn't run-of-the mill, and that is definitely stimulating and entertaining, try Martyrs and Manifestation. . . ."
—Tammy Ruggles for *Readers' Favorite*

"Engaging storytelling . . . bursts with odd, witty, playful incidents and characters. The narrative continually surprises . . . charming . . . laugh-out-loud funny."

— The BookLife Prize by *Publishers Weekly*
for Book Two of the Candlewicke 13 Series.

"Whether you're a younger reader or just young at heart, this is a very immersive, high-quality fantasy series that never ceases to amaze me with its imaginative quality and new twists to the plot."

— K.C. Finn for *Readers' Favorite*

"Vibrant and funny. . . ." — The Booklife Prize by *Publishers Weekly*
for Book One of the Candlewicke 13 Series.

www.ingramcontent.com/pod-product-compliance
Lightning Source LLC
Chambersburg PA
CBHW021309190726
48288CB00003B/765